We Wa

By Bill Hiatt

With cover art by
Peter O'Connor,
Bespoke Book Covers

Dedication

This book is dedicated to the Beverly Hills High School English Department. On dark days my fellow English teachers were often my light.

What Has Gone Before

We Walk in Darkness is the fifth book in the Spell Weaver series. If you are interested in reading the previous books first, you can find their titles in "The Adventure Isn't Over." However, if you can't wait to read this book, I have tried to include in the text enough information about earlier events in the Spell Weaver series to make it possible for someone new to the series to understand and enjoy the adventures in this book without having read the earlier ones. In fact, this book is probably the closest to being a stand-alone work since the first book in the series.

CONTENTS

Chapter 1: Prelude (Umbra)

"Umbra!" snapped the Praeceptor. "Enough of these senseless questions!"

As always, though I could barely see her, I could hear her clearly. My ability to see without light still required some distinction to work, and she was virtually indistinguishable from the shadows that surrounded us both.

"I ask your pardon, Praeceptor," I replied with what I hoped was the right amount of humility, "but I did not raise the question out of idle curiosity. My physical form is not as well-suited to the work. I thought perhaps if I understood why I was not like the others—"

I saw what might have been an impatient wave of an arm in the darkness to my left.

"Your physical form is adequate to the purpose, or you would not have been chosen for training," the Praeceptor replied. "That is all you need to know."

"My skin is so much paler though. Will I not be more visible in the darkness?"

She sighed. "The proper application of shadow magic will still conceal you, and there may actually be times when your appearance will be an advantage."

"I understand, Praeceptor." I wasn't really satisfied, but I knew that was as much answer as I would get. Pressing further would only make her angry, and I knew from experience how much I did not want the Praeceptor to be angry with me.

"That is well," she replied, "for your training is nearly at its end, and you will soon begin your trials."

Her touch chilled my left arm. "I cannot stress enough the importance of performing well. Your failure would not reflect well on me, and...there would be no further use for you."

She did not need to tell me what that meant. If I had no further use, my existence would be ended.

"I will do what is required," I said. Had I said more, my voice might have shaken just a little, and then the Praeceptor would have lectured me again about the importance of emotional control.

"Your first trial involves a human," she said.

A human? That made no sense to me. I was afraid to speak but decided I had to take the chance. I had to know the nature of the trial if I was to succeed.

"Would our real targets ever be human? Wouldn't our services be needed more for someone not so easily killed?"

The Praeceptor laughed, but the sound conveyed contempt rather than amusement. "Our services are needed wherever a dominus says they are needed, and have I not told you a thousand times? Never underestimate a target. The subject of your trial is human, yes, but he has certain unusual skills. We suspect he may have some faerie ancestry. I will tell you all that is known of him before the trial begins. Remember one thing: the trials will never pit you against someone you could dispatch too easily. What would be the point of that?"

"I understand, Praeceptor," I replied, though in truth I still did not. A human who was part faerie? I had never heard of such a thing. From what I had been taught, humans had no special skills that one of us would need to fear.

"In that case, we are nearly done for today," said the Praeceptor. "Recite the affirmation for me, and your lesson will be at an end."

There, at least, was a task that raised no questions I did not know how to answer. "We walk in darkness, for light is death to us. We strike in darkness, for we cannot be seen. We kill in darkness, for that is our purpose, and without purpose we ourselves would die."

I had known those words for as long as I could remember. Usually they comforted me, but not today. Today I had questions the affirmation alone could not banish.

Chapter 2: Strange Shadows (Lucas)

"Hey, Twinkle Toes, wait up!" yelled Gavin, running to catch up with me.

I walked faster on purpose. Yeah, he was my best friend, but that didn't mean I had to put up with the nickname.

Predictably, Gavin, as fast in everyday life as he was on the football field or the baseball diamond, caught up with me without breaking a sweat. "Uh, sorry, man. I forgot you don't like me to call you that. You don't have to ignore me."

"You're too big to ignore anyway, Goliath," I said with a chuckle.

He winced. Apparently, nicknames were OK as long as they didn't apply to him.

"Truce!" he said, holding up his hands, and I nodded. After all, best friends did get to annoy each other from time to time—and we'd been best friends so long we might as well have been twin brothers. In all that time, though, I never told Gavin why the nicknames bothered me.

It wasn't because I was the star of our high school's dance program. Whatever self-consciousness I might have had about dancing—and it's hard for a guy to be a dancer in high school, believe me—faded away when I started capoeira. I had Dad to thank for that, although when he said I could pursue dance as long as I also did a martial art, I doubt he had capoeira in mind. I could have resented his insistence on martial arts, since it clearly suggested that there was something wrong with just being a dancer and that I had to balance it out with something more traditionally masculine. Instead of reacting hostilely, though, I found a martial art so closely related to dance that the two disciplines would reinforce each other. As an added bonus, because capoeira was Brazilian and so were we, Dad couldn't object too loudly; after all, I was just exploring my cultural roots.

In any case, any frustration he might have had over my choice faded as I progressed rapidly through the cord levels (like belts in other martial arts). There were several different cord systems, but my *mestre* used the one created by Confederacao Brasileira de Capoeira. Under that system, at the last *batizado* I had been awarded the *verde amarelo azul* (green, yellow, and blue) cord of the *formado*, the first of the advanced levels. Higher levels had to be earned by teaching capoeira as well as practicing it. *Mestre* Ribeiro had made a big deal out of the fact that he had never had a student progress as fast as I had. My parents both beamed at that, and I knew my dad would never hassle me about dance again.

Actually, no one gave me grief about dance since the day two years ago when I efficiently dealt with a couple of bullies who thought the dancing sissy would be an easy mark. I used restraint, so neither one of them ended up in the hospital...but they did come close.

So no, I wasn't uncomfortable with being a dancer. I was uncomfortable with the fact that I was a freak.

Around twelve, when I first started puberty, I began to experience visions of some kind—not hallucinations, but genuine psychic events. One of the first was seeing Gavin get injured in a middle-school football game before he actually did. I had the vision only a minute or so before the actual event, not really in time to warn him, and that was usually the way those visions seemed to work. It was like my mind somehow fast-forwarded just enough to see what was right ahead, and then moved back into the present. I never told anyone about this, not even Gavin. Being able to do that kind of thing made me feel strange. The fact that it was a basically useless ability didn't help.

I didn't go glassy-eyed or anything while I was having visions, so they were easy to cover up. Not so easy to hide was my speed. Also when I was around twelve, I discovered that I could move faster than a normal guy. I don't mean comic-book-superhero fast, but fast enough to make a dance choreographer pause and blink, fast enough to cause *Mestre* Ribeiro to do a double-take. As soon as I realized what was happening, I restrained myself, but that kind of self-discipline wasn't easy, especially during high adrenalin moments. The temptation to dominate at capoeira was sometimes nearly overwhelming.

I didn't exactly expect people to take me out and burn me at the stake. I didn't actually know what to expect. But I already stuck out like a sore thumb in a small central California town with a good share of rednecks. Aside from being a male dancer, I was Hispanic with an African American best friend. I was dark-skinned and dark-haired enough to have been told to go back where I came from more than once. You wouldn't think I'd get that in a predominately Hispanic county, but I did. I could only imagine what would happen if people found out I was...well, that was another problem. Even I didn't know what I was.

Alien (I mean the extraterrestrial kind)? Mutant? Changeling? I had no clue.

My doctor hadn't noticed anything out of the ordinary during my annual physicals. Probably just as well, but I would have liked to know what was up with me…as long as I could keep that knowledge to myself.

Gavin and I were approaching the diner on Main Street, and since dance rehearsal had run long, as had Gavin's baseball practice, we both should have probably headed home. However, Gavin, who ate like food was about to go out of style, wanted to stop and get some fries. His metabolism was so fast, I half expected him to starve walking home from school—or at least, his complaints about how hungry he was would give me that impression. How could I say no to a friend in need?

Gavin opened the door, and I was hit by a blast of air conditioning, which felt pretty good after a day that could easily have fit July, though we had barely started April. (Our town's a little east of Merced; think Merced, but even hotter—and Merced sometimes gets to ninety degrees in the shade before summer even starts.)

What didn't feel so good was the sudden, sharp feeling that we shouldn't stay there, that we needed to go home. Either Mom had started sending me psychic broadcasts, or this was another one of my premonitions, though this time there was no actual vision, just a feeling.

I looked around quickly. Traffic on Main Street was pretty minimal, with no sign of an impending drive-by shooting or anything like that. The interior of the diner didn't look threatening, either.

"Lucas!" shouted Sally, the diner's owner, from inside. "Come in, or go out. I don't want to pay to air condition the great out of doors!"

"Sorry." I stepped inside, with Gavin right behind me. That was the last thing that I wanted to do, but I couldn't very well tell Gavin that I was getting a psychic red alert of some kind, and I couldn't think fast enough to come up a decent excuse that would get me out of there.

I steered us to a booth with a good window view of the street and a view of the front door, though how much that would help if someone did a drive-by shooting or barged in with guns blazing, I didn't know.

The diner wasn't too busy, so our duplicate orders of fries and a Coke appeared pretty fast. I was all about finishing everything so we could leave, but Gavin, who usually ate like a giant piranha, was uncharacteristically slow, pushing each fry through the ketchup like he was trying to dig a hole in his plate.

"Lucas, what's up?" Gavin finally asked. I guessed my fidgeting was unnerving him.

I made a big show of checking the time. "Uh, I think my mom plans on serving dinner around seven thirty, and it's that now, that's all."

Gavin grinned. "Yeah, I guess I didn't even notice the sun setting...but I thought you told me your dad wouldn't be home until eight tonight."

That was the problem with having a friend who knew me too well. Gavin actually remembered my dad's schedule even though I had forgotten it.

I faked a quick smile. "You're right. Dance rehearsal was so hard today that I must have blown out a few brain cells."

His eyes narrowed a little. "Lucas, I've seen you in dance...and in capoeira. It never looks hard for you."

"Looks can be deceiving," I said, trying to sound casual as I motioned the waitress for the check.

"Nothing's wrong, is it?" Aside from knowing my dad's schedule better than I did, Gavin could read me better than a seismologist could read a Richter scale.

"Nah, G, it's all good," I lied. "I'm just nervous for no reason."

"OK. Just checking." He put down his share of the check and tip, clearly taking the hint that I wanted to leave.

I did the same, and I breathed a sigh of relief as we got out of the diner without incident. Evidently my psychic powers were off this time. There still wasn't a sign of trouble in any direction as I said goodbye to Gavin and we went our separate ways.

The diner was right on the boundary between the tiny business district and a small web of residential streets that curved gently away from the center of town. Madisonville (or Hicksville, as I tended to refer to it in private), was the result of some developers noticing a little vacant land and saying to themselves, "Why not put a town here?" I think my parents said something about it being intended as a bedroom community for people who worked in Merced, and indeed, practically all of my friends' parents commuted every day to one of the surrounding areas.

Merced at least had history. Madisonville, conjured up strictly for economic reasons, never felt as if it had a soul. Everything was relatively new, including our house—and pretty much every other house in town, as far as that was concerned. We lived in a nice two-story, but, to maximize profit, the developers squeezed as many houses as they could into a relatively confined space. The result was that most of the houses, mine included, had backyards so small and narrow that if you put in a hot tub, no one could walk from one end of the yard to the other without wading part of the way.

I was about halfway home when I noticed something odd. I was surrounded by what passed for darkness in Western society, but, of course, there was always enough electric light to keep the sky from being totally dark, and the street I was walking down, like every other street in town, had its share of streetlights. Still, there were some shadowy areas, mostly along the sides of houses. I was used to that.

What I wasn't used to was the way a shadow seemed to have detached itself from its surroundings and started following me. That could have been an optical illusion of some kind, but I was getting another jolt of psychic warning, still not a vision, but the strongest warning I'd ever felt. Even the time I almost got hit by a car wasn't this intense.

Nonetheless, I resisted the urge to run screaming down the street. Instead, I blinked a couple of times, and the wandering shadow seemed to disappear. The feeling didn't though. Something was just not right. I might not like having these psychic nudges, but I'll say this for them: they had never been wrong.

Getting home seemed to be the best plan. I still had a ten-minute walk. My muscles were sore from dance, but I ignored their protest as I sped up. Instead of fading, though, the feeling of foreboding grew more overwhelming.

What's the best way to get out of trouble when you don't know what the trouble is and can't ask for help? I could just imagine what calling nine-one-one would be like. "Yeah, officer, I just had a feeling something bad was about to happen." nine-one-one operators deserve a good laugh as much as anybody, but I wasn't about to provide it if I could help it.

I was near enough to my house that I knew several of the families who lived in the area, but I couldn't think fast enough to develop an excuse for just dropping in.

I was about two blocks from my house, and the psychic alarm bells were deafening…but why? I was running toward safety…wasn't I? What I needed was a vision, but I still had only the feeling.

Ahead and to my left, a shadow flickered away from the flowering cherry tree I thought was casting it and glided in my direction. Either I was crazy, or the shadow was stalking me—and now it was between me and home.

I thought about circling back, but the shadow was picking up speed and was almost upon me.

Still not knowing what I was dealing with, I turned and ran, abandoning all restraint and accelerating to full speed, praying no one was looking out the window as I blasted past.

After a block I risked turning enough to see if the shadow was following. It was, though I had put a little more distance between us. As far as I could tell, it moved pretty fast, but it didn't glide after me in a straight line. Instead, it zigzagged, staying away from the areas lit most clearly by the streetlights.

A little more confident now that I could outrun it, I turned at the next cross street, ran down it, and started up the next street, once again headed for my house. All I would have to do was keep far enough ahead of the shadow, cross back onto my street at the next intersection, and I should be fine.

Except that as I approached the next intersection, the shadow appeared again—in front of me. Either there was more than one of the things, or it had some nonlinear method of getting from point A to point B. Either way, I was pretty much screwed.

I still had no idea what I was dealing with. Obviously, whatever was chasing me wasn't just a shadow, but, aside from that, I knew nothing. I would have been sure it was some kind of weird hallucination, optical illusion, or maybe even an eye problem, except for the nonstop howling of my personal alarm system. I knew instinctively that letting the shadow catch me would be bad—very bad.

I'd probably be safe if I just went into somebody's house, and I knew at least a couple people on this block, but I still hadn't had any inspiration on how to drop in without looking like a complete idiot. I was sweating profusely and breathing heavily, so a mundane, "I think I left my notebook in English; did you pick it up?" wasn't going to cut it.

However, "I've been running from the shadows and needed a rest," clearly wasn't an option either.

I finally settled for the stereotypic insecure teenager move and ran all the way back to Main Street instead of making myself look like a moron in front of one of my friends. The trip was a much longer trip than it should have been, since I had to make several switchbacks to avoid the shadow. The grocery store on Main was small but had really bright lighting, so I thought maybe the shadow couldn't follow me in.

I must have been looking pretty disheveled by that point, because the night clerk immediately gave me the evil eye. Checking my reflection in the glass of one of the refrigerated displays, I did a little repair work with a comb and tried to get my breathing back to normal. In the past few minutes, I'd piled up a pretty big oxygen debt, and I was still more panting than breathing.

My cell phone vibrated in my pocket, and I quickly checked it. Mom, as I might have guessed. During my little marathon, I'd missed three of her calls. It had been almost an hour since I'd left the diner, Dad was home, and we had unexpected company. In a polite, mom sort of way, she had left messages asking where the hell I was, each more concerned than the last.

I looked out the large window in the front of the store. Sure enough, if I looked closely, I saw a shadow defying the normal laws of science, hovering just outside the range of light from the store but still clearly visible...well, at least to me. It occurred to me that perhaps my psychic senses were involved. Even if I had the guts to point out to people that a shadow was following me, I wondered if any of them would see it.

I thought about calling home and using a twisted ankle or something like that as an excuse to have Dad come and pick me up. I was sure he would...but what if the shadow went for him when he got here? I still didn't know what I was dealing with.

I had never before tried to have a vision. I wasn't sure I could provoke one, but I had to make the attempt. If I knew what was after me and what it wanted, maybe I could work out a way out of this mess. Otherwise, all I could think to do was run down to the all-night drugstore and stay there until dawn—a move the night clerk there wouldn't be happy with. Neither would my parents.

My phone vibrated again. Again I didn't answer.

I closed my eyes and tried to remember what it was like to have a vision, the split-second of disorientation, the momentary fast-forward into a vivid glimpse of something in the future. Then I tried to duplicate that feeling, to drag my mind into the same state.

Nothing. Absolutely nothing.

I opened my eyes and jumped. I guessed I had been so focused I didn't hear someone walk up to me.

The bad news: the night clerk—that little weasel—had called the cops on me. The good news: the responding officer was a friend of my dad's.

"Sorry, son," he said in his deep voice, "I didn't mean to scare you."

"It's OK, Officer Sullivan. I'm just having a bad night. I was having a run, but I twisted my ankle, and now I have a headache too."

Officer Sullivan looked at me appraisingly. "The clerk said you've been loitering."

"I'm sorry about that. I've just been trying to work up my nerve to call my parents. I'm kind of embarrassed by the whole ankle thing, but I don't think I can walk far enough on it to get home."

"It's a pretty slow night," observed Sullivan. In a town like ours, I imagined most nights were pretty slow for the police. "Why don't I drive you home?"

That offer created another dilemma. Obviously Sullivan had gotten in without being attacked, but might the shadow go for him if we came out together? I had no way of knowing, but I suspected if I turned down a ride, the best case scenario was that he'd call my dad, who would end up being exposed to the shadow, or Sullivan would take me down to the station, in which case he would be exposed anyway. Call me selfish, but if someone was going to be at risk regardless, I didn't want it to be my dad. I might as well go for the alternative that stood the best chance of working well if the shadow didn't attack.

"Thanks, Officer. If it's no trouble, I'd appreciate a lift." Being sure to affect a distinct limp, I hobbled past the clerk, who eyed me sullenly. I stepped out the door with Sullivan right behind and headed for the police cruiser. I longed to race to it, but I'd blow my twisted-ankle cover if I did. Fortunately, I saw no sign of misbehaving shadows, and we both got into the car with no problem.

The drive home took a few minutes. I made lame small talk with Sullivan while I stared out the car window, checking for any sign of unusual shadow activity. There didn't seem to be any, so either it couldn't keep up with a car, or it didn't want to attack while somebody else was around.

When we got close, I asked Sullivan to let me out at the end of the block.

"Your ankle—" he began.

"Thanks, but I can make it part of a block. You know what my parents will think if I pull up in a squad car."

He chuckled. "Yeah, you're probably right, but be careful of that ankle."

"Will do, and thanks, Officer."

He nodded, and I made a show of being wobbly when I got out of the car. I must have done too good a job, because the car followed me down the street until I started hobbling up the walkway to my own front porch. Normally, something like that might have annoyed me, but tonight I was actually glad he did it. After all, what would I have done if he'd driven away, and the shadow pounced on me again?

Actually, fending off the shadow might have been easier than fending off my mom, who came bursting out the front door and met me halfway between the house and the sidewalk.

"*Filho*, what happened? You worried me half to death!" she said, giving me her sternest expression.

"I'm sorry, *Mãe*. I decided to run part of the way home and twisted my ankle. I just now found a ride home." I hated like hell to lie to her, but I couldn't very well tell her what really happened. Then I noticed she was wearing her best dress, and her hair was pulled back in the way she did when Dad took her out to dinner. The reference to company in her messages popped back into my mind.

"We're having company tonight?" I asked.

"If you saw my messages, why didn't you reply?" she asked, clearly upset. "And yes, your *avó* is here, all the way from Brazil. What is she going to think when her *neto* is this late?"

The news that the Brazilian grandmother I had never met was here wasn't quite as shocking as being attacked by shadows, but it was almost as much of a surprise—and not a welcome one. I had way too much to worry about already. Trying to make a good impression on someone who was a stranger to me in every way except genetically was the last thing I needed.

Mom hustled me toward the door, and I had to remind myself to limp unless I wanted to be exposed as a complete liar. Usually so caring, Mom didn't even seem to notice. Her reaction suggested I had a very traditional, very difficult grandmother who would be instantly critical.

Imagine my surprise when we got inside and the woman who greeted me looked a lot less like the family matriarch and a lot more like someone ready to go clubbing in Rio with men a third her age. Oh, she was clearly older than Mom, though I never would have guessed old enough to be her mother, and it was certainly hard to visualize this woman as anyone's grandmother. I had to look closely to notice what little gray hid in her black hair; my parents actually had more than she did. Finding any wrinkles was even more taxing, though I thought I detected one or two very faint marks on her brown skin.

"*Neto*!" she said happily, embracing me before I could protest.

"*Avó*, I'm all sweaty!" I said apologetically.

"Men sweat," she said, almost approvingly. Then she let go of me and looked me up and down.

"And a man is clearly what you are, Lucas. Your parents must be very proud."

She cut off my dad with the last part. He was clearly about to scold me for getting home so late and not calling. I had always thought of him as a dynamic presence, but he seemed much less so in the presence of my grandmother.

"Uh, yes, we are very proud," he said diplomatically. "Lucas, why don't you wash up for dinner?" I took the hint and limped upstairs for a quick shower.

Dinner started out better than I expected. Even though Mom obviously hadn't anticipated any visitors, or she would have told me this morning, she had somehow managed to whip up her best *galeto* (roasted chicken), with a nice serving of rice and beans and an elaborate dessert I couldn't name, though mango and coconut were both involved somehow. Since our menu was American most nights, I had to think that Mom had prepared all of this more or less last minute, and I was surprised she hadn't been more upset by my lateness, which could have ruined everything.

Grandmother—hard as it was to think of her as one—dominated the conversation, which I think annoyed Dad a little, but Mom, who seemed to have expected something like that to happen, took the whole thing in stride.

Anyway, the woman extracted so much information from me that a military interrogator would have been impressed by her thoroughness. Probably because we'd never met, she couldn't really know that much about me, and she clearly wanted to fill that void…all in one night, apparently. Not only that, but she seemed interested in everything. Usually, my other grandparents asked polite questions, but they weren't all that interested in teenage stuff like what kind of music I listened to. Not so *Avó*, who listened carefully to the answer to every question, seemingly enthralled by details of pop culture most people of her generation couldn't have cared less about. She was even more interested in my dancing, and she soaked up every word about capoeira.

"It is good you can defend yourself," she said at one point. "You never know when you might have to."

Given the fact that a couple hours earlier my life might have been in danger, that choice of subject seemed weirdly coincidental. Equally weird was the way my mom glared at her when she said it.

"Capoeira does look like it takes a lot of skill," observed Dad, "but I think I'd prefer something like karate for actual self-defense."

Avó looked at him as if he had just announced that Lichtenstein could beat the United States in a war. "I have seen a skilled capoeirista defeat three armed men and have heard of situations in which even more adversaries were vanquished at one time. I know nothing of karate, but I find it hard to imagine it could be any more effective."

"Wouldn't it be unwise, though, for someone like Lucas to try taking on armed men?" asked my dad in a tone that suggested he was trying to cue *Avó* on what the correct response would be.

"Only a fool seeks violence, but sometimes there is no other way," replied *Avó*, missing her cue by a mile.

Sensing a potential conflict, Mom, moving about as fast as I'd ever seen her move, served the adults *cachaça*, a Brazilian liquor made from sugarcane. That move didn't help as much as she might have anticipated, however, because then *Avó* asked, "Shouldn't Lucas have some, too? He's a man now, after all."

"He's below the legal drinking age…even in Brazil, I believe," said my dad in a way that made the room feel about ten degrees cooler.

"I think I've heard that in California a parent may serve a son or daughter alcohol legally," replied *Avó* smoothly.

"I'm fine, *Avó*," I said. "I need to keep myself in the best possible physical shape for dance and for capoeira. It's like I'm…in training."

"Well, I can't argue with your dedication," said *Avó*, looking straight at me as if Dad wasn't in the room any more. "I would imagine you would like to keep yourself in the best possible shape for the ladies as well, yes?"

My other grandparents occasionally asked about girlfriends, but there was something almost suggestive in *Avó's* tone, something that made me blush.

"Mother!" said Mom abruptly.

"He's a handsome young man, and surely there are women who desire him…" *Avó* fell silent in response to Mom's continued glare.

OK, now I was officially weirded out. Unless I was just imagining things, the way *Avó* said "desire" seemed overly direct and loaded with innuendo. While I pondered her tone, she caught my eye and winked at me in a very ungrandmotherly way, almost like another guy would have done. The whole situation reminded me of one of those movies in which an alien is trying to impersonate a human and not doing a particularly good job of it.

"Please forgive me," said *Avó*, still talking to me and not to my dad, though I sensed Mom was part of her intended audience. "I'm afraid I don't really know any teenagers, and I haven't much practice in talking to them. I certainly didn't mean to embarrass you."

"You didn't," I lied. I glanced at Dad, who looked livid, but *Avó* was his mother-in-law, and he must have decided not to say anything as long as she was backing off anyway.

To break the awkward silence, I did talk a little—in very parent-friendly terms—about the girls I had dated. *Avó* listened intently but said almost nothing. My mom continually giving her the evil eye might have had something to do with that.

I excused myself shortly after that and went up to my room, now thoroughly tense. There was something wrong; that was for sure—and not just with shadows coming alive and menacing me, though that by itself would have been enough.

Relatives who lived close might pop by for an unannounced visit, but who pops by all the way from Brazil? For all *Avó* knew, we might not even have been in town; Dad sometimes traveled for business, and we had just gotten back from spring break, though she could have checked my school calendar on the Internet. Then there was her conversation, which had seemed less and less grandmotherly as dinner progressed, becoming more and more like that of a mischievous older sister. As the robot on the old TV show *Lost in Space* used to say, "It does not compute!"

I probably would have brooded longer over all the strangeness, but I was more exhausted than I remembered ever being. Spending all that time running after a strenuous dance workout obviously took more out of me than I had realized at first. Luckily, I had finished my homework before dance, so I focused on stilling my mind enough to sleep.

Just as I switched off my light and was about to crawl into bed, I had a vision, the kind I would have killed to have had earlier. Unlike my typical vision, though, this one seemed mundane and nonthreatening, just *Avó* and Mom out in the kitchen having coffee and talking. I held my breath, expecting some sudden catastrophe, but nothing happened. Then I listened more carefully to what they were saying, and suddenly the vision became a lot less mundane.

"You have to be more careful, Gabriela!" cautioned Mom. Odd! As liberal as *Avó* seemed to be, I had a hard time imagining Mom being raised to call her mother by her first name.

"I'm sure I don't know what you mean," replied *Avó* defensively.

"I mean you have to stop acting like some...bohemian and start acting more like a grandmother. Lucas is a smart boy. For that matter, his father's very sharp as well. Neither one of them will buy this grandmother act unless you do it more convincingly."

Grandmother act?

"I wouldn't have had to do it at all if you had been able to follow simple instructions. I told you to get Lucas out of here. I told you there was danger."

"I could never have explained to Paulo," Mom said.

Avó—or whoever she really was—snorted. "Men are born to be managed. Don't tell me you couldn't have thought of some way to convince your husband, Carolina." Again I picked up the vibe of unspoken innuendo.

"I don't *manage* my husband; I love him."

"Much good that will do him when his son is dead."

When his son is dead?

"We don't even know the danger is real," insisted Mom.

Avó raised an eyebrow. "Don't we? I'm sure I smelled fear on Lucas the moment he came in. That twisted ankle nonsense was just a cover. Something happened this very night."

"Why wouldn't he say something?" asked Mom, her voice shaking a little.

"For the same reason you've never told him the truth: he has no way to explain what happened, and he doesn't think you'll believe him. We should go upstairs this minute and tell him everything!"

You've never told him the truth?

"Paulo—" began Mom.

"Is sleeping soundly," said *Avó*, "and will continue to do so until I wake him."

I was numb, unable to figure out how to react. *Avó* was an impostor. Dad was "asleep"—drugged probably. There was a truth Mom had never told me.

And I had been running from shadows! Clearly they were the least of my worries.

Chapter 3: Fighting Shadows (Lucas)

Looking at the kitchen clock in my vision and comparing it to the glowing face of my alarm in my room, I realized that this vision, in contrast to my earlier ones, was of the present. If I wanted to, I could go downstairs and join right in, demanding to know who *Avó* really was and what the truth was that Mom had kept from me.

Then again, the impostor *Avó* had drugged Dad. What if she was dangerous?

Great! First running from shadows, and now worrying whether I could take my impostor grandmother.

At the moment, I had on boxers, hardly the right attire for a conversation with two women. I quickly got into tomorrow's school clothes and moved as quietly as I could down the hall, and then down the stairs. Their muffled voices, quiet but intense, came from the kitchen. I could have made a run for the front door, but there was one thing I knew for sure. Crazy as the circumstances were, Mom was still Mom—at least, I hoped she was. After a moment's hesitation I hung a right and walked straight into the kitchen.

The two women could hardly have been more surprised, but they covered well.

"Lucas, couldn't you sleep?" asked Mom. "Do you want some warm milk or something?"

"What I want," I said, pulling out one of the chairs at the kitchen table and sitting in it, "is the truth."

Avó played it cool, but Mom paled immediately. "I…I don't know what you mean. Truth?"

"I heard you guys talking," I said, trying to keep my voice level. Turning to *Avó*, I said, "I know you aren't my grandmother." Turning back to Mom, I continued, "I know you've been keeping a secret from me."

"I was going to tell you as soon as you turned eighteen," said Mom, looking back and forth between me and *Avó* as if she were trapped between us.

"The proverbial cat is out of the bag…and doing the samba," observed *Avó* in an incongruously upbeat tone. "You may as well tell him now. Perhaps knowing will help him accept what must be done."

Far from picking up the suggestion, Mom stared at *Avó* as if my pretend grandmother had just shot her through the heart.

Looking exasperated, *Avó* turned to me and said, "I suppose the truth-telling falls to me, *Neto*!"

"Don't call me that!" I snapped. "You don't have the right."

Avó jerked back as if I had slapped her, as if she really were my grandmother. "You will feel differently once you have the whole tale...*Bisneto*," she said gently.

"You think I'm stupid?" I asked bitterly. "You don't even look old enough to be my grandmother. Great-grandmother? Really?"

"Lucas—" began Mom tentatively.

"You didn't want to tell," interrupted...my great-grandmother? *Bisavó*? Strange as this evening had been so far, I wasn't about to buy that nonsense.

"Now it's my turn," continued the impostor, looking away from Mom and toward me. "I am...older than I appear to be. I could, in fact, appear any age I choose."

"Gabriela!" said my mom urgently. "I know what you're thinking, but don't! It would be too much of a shock for him."

"What is that old saying?" asked...Gabriela? I was having a hard time deciding what to call her.

"Ah, yes!" she continued triumphantly. "One picture is worth a thousand words." She waved her arm, and my vision rippled for a moment, I blinked, and suddenly it was not the lively Gabriela sitting in front of me but an ancient woman, her face as wrinkled as a raisin, her withered scalp covered by only a few wisps of white hair, her back bent from osteoporosis. Then, with a wave of a shriveled arm, she made that ripple in my vision again, and just as abruptly as the old woman appeared, she was gone—replaced by a beautiful girl my age, with jet-black hair, skin like caramel, and a curving figure that would have given me ideas if not for the possibility that I might be related to her. Another wave of the arm, and the woman who had introduced herself as *Avó* was back.

I looked at Mom accusingly. "You...you drugged me! You gave me some kind of hallucinogen at dinner!"

Gabriela...or *Avó*...or *Bisavó*...or whoever she was, looked amused. "Why would she have, *Bisneto*? In case you overheard us talking, and we needed to convince you of some wild story? And if she had, how could she get a drug to show you exactly what we wanted you to see?"

"Hypnotic suggestion, then," I said stubbornly, looking suspiciously at both of them.

To my surprise, the mystery woman in front of me laughed, glanced my mom's way, and said, "Too many spy novels!" To me she said, "Honestly, Lucas, the truth is so much less complicated than the stories you're inventing. I *am* your great-grandmother, I can change my appearance at will, and I can do other forms of magic...as can any of the Encantado."

"Encantado?" I said, my mind momentarily blank. Then I remembered those childhood stories. "You want me to believe those fairy tales Mom told me when I was a little kid—creatures like dolphins who live in an undersea world called the Encante and assume human form from time to time to..." I had to think for a minute to remember exactly why.

"Yes, Lucas," said Mom, trying for a matter-of-fact tone and not quite making it. "Sometimes an Encantado entered the human world because he or she fell in love with a human being."

"Since we're being honest, that's the kiddie version," said the mystery woman. "In the beginning, it was usually much more about making love than being in love."

If the woman really had been my grandmother, that would have been a colossal overshare if ever there was one.

"Don't worry," she continued. "Though your great-grandfather was a magnificent lover, our relationship quickly became more than just sexual."

Again, more than I really wanted to know. I had to keep reminding myself that none of it could possibly be true.

The only thing I knew for sure was that I had to get out of here. They must have given me something, maybe a drug that made me subject to suggestion. The mystery woman put the idea of being able to alter her appearance in my mind. Yeah, that was it. They had certainly drugged Dad to keep him out of the way...but out of the way of what? I didn't want to stick around to find out.

Neither one of the women appeared armed, but I wasn't sure I wanted a physical confrontation anyway. I had never hit a woman, let alone my own mother—assuming she really was my mother. I could no longer be sure even of that. My best bet was to run like hell, put some distance between me and them, and then use my cell to call the police. Crazy as my story would sound to any sane officer, there were probably still traces of something in my blood, and Dad was still out cold—that they could easily check. If I was lucky, Sullivan would still be on duty.

The kitchen wasn't exactly set up for capoeira, but I worked with what I had. In one fluid motion I stood, threw the chair in such a way that it would block Mom's path, and launched myself through the door, not troubling to conceal my freakish speed.

"Lucas!" Mom yelled after me. "You're in danger!"

I was already at the front door. I flicked open the deadbolt and reached for the chain, which became a green snake with angry eyes and enormous fangs. The hallucinogen again! I forced myself to ignore what I was seeing and get the chain unlatched. For a second, I thought I was trapped; it's pretty hard to work with objects you can't really see. Then the snake disappeared. I got the chain off, and I threw the door open. I got out just before the women reached me.

Then I froze, closer to complete panic than I had ever been in my life. Shocked out of disciplined thinking by the betrayal within my own family, I had momentarily forgotten about the shadow. It had not forgotten about me.

Even from a quick glance, I saw it moving just beyond the glow of the porch light. Then I realized I couldn't really be seeing it. The street was abnormally dark. Somehow, I could still see its movement, though. Perhaps whatever weird psychic ability I had let me perceive the shadow better than I should have been able to.

Why was the street so dark? In another second I realized what had happened. Somehow every single streetlight on the block had gone out. Maybe every one had been broken. I thought I caught the glint of broken glass on the sidewalk. Not that it mattered how the thing had put the streetlights out, only that it had. If I tried to make a run for it, the shadow could follow me much faster than it had when it had kept out of the glow closest to the streetlights.

"Come inside, Lucas!"

I jumped despite myself.

During the moments I had hesitated, the mystery woman had come up right behind me.

I spun to face her. "Stay back! I don't want to hurt you, but I will if I have to." Whether I really would, I didn't know, but I was hoping she wasn't willing to risk calling my bluff. If all else failed, I could start yelling bloody murder, and someone was bound to call nine-one-one.

"I don't want to hurt you either," she said quietly, probably trying to avoid attracting attention from the neighbors. "I came to protect you, which I can do much better inside the house. You can accept my help, or you can stand here, with your back turned on one of the *pessoas da sombra,* until it figures out a way to kill you despite the porch light.

My Portuguese was a little rusty, but I knew what she meant: people of the shadow. Somehow, she knew, or at least had made an educated guess about what was after me.

There's an old saying, "Better the devil you know than the devil you don't." Wise words, but how could I apply them when I didn't know either devil?

"Lucas, please!" Mom, assuming that's who she really was, had joined us.

I did know her, even if I couldn't figure out why she had brought a stranger into our house, drugged Dad, drugged me.

I glanced at the shadow. Its shape was roughly human, and its arm movement suggested it was about to throw something.

"We can't—" the mystery woman began. The rock whizzed past, and a second later, glass broke. Suddenly, the only light came from the still open front door.

The damn thing had taken out the porch light!

Had I been alone, I would have just run back into the house, slammed the door, and called the police. I couldn't tell them a shadow was after me, but I could tell them some punk kid was out throwing rocks at streetlights and porch lights. In Madisonville, that was the equivalent of a major crime spree, and the police would come, with car headlights, and flashlights—lots of flashlights—and the thing might retreat.

The problem was that I wasn't alone, and if I went into the house, the women would be with me. I didn't trust the mystery woman at all, and, right now I didn't trust Mom much, either. If I couldn't retreat, there was only one other choice. Reflexively I moved into the *ginga,* the basic foot-movement pattern of capoeira. Assuming the shadow wanted me specifically and wouldn't dash around me to get to them, they could retreat into the house…and would, if they had any sense.

One of the basic principles of capoeira is to keep moving in a pattern that could confuse an opponent and make hitting the capoeirista much more difficult. There really was something to the old adage that it's harder to strike a moving target, particularly one moving at faster than human speed. The women had already seen how quickly I could move, as had the shadow, so there was no point in holding back now.

The thing moved closer, trying to stay in the shadow thrown by my body, which blocked the light from the door. I used the *ginga* to unexpectedly hit the thing with light every few seconds, and each time it backed up again. This might be easier than I thought.

Then I realized the women were still behind me. I wanted to focus on the fight without having to worry about them.

"Get inside the house!" I demanded.

"If you insist on staying in danger, I'm staying with you," Mom whispered.

I didn't look back, but I guessed her eyes were on the impossibly moving shadow.

"Though it would be better if we all got out of danger," pointed out the mystery woman.

As I continued the *ginga*, the conversation continued behind me—much to my annoyance. Now that I was facing the thing more calmly than when it had first attacked, I became increasingly confident I could figure out how to beat it…if only I didn't have to worry about bystanders.

"Gabriela, can't you do something?" whispered Mom.

"I don't think the illusion of light will stop it," the mystery woman whispered back, "and I doubt it would be affected by my illusions anyway. I might test it, though, just to see."

I used every ounce of self-discipline I had to block out the conversation. I couldn't make them leave, but if they were behind me and closer to the light, they could be relatively safe. If I could defeat the shadow, I could make all of us safe, hopefully for good.

However, as I kept moving, and the shadow kept twitching as if it were trying to figure out my pattern, I had to wonder how I could beat it. Did it have some kind of physical presence? I guessed if it could attack me, it had to have some form of real-world body, and it was clear that the thing was sensitive to light, not that that helped. Capoeira had a lot of interesting moves, but none of them could generate light. I hoped a good solid blow would work. The only alternative was to run back into the house with someone I hoped was my mom and someone I knew was a stranger I didn't trust...and, given the shadow's ingenuity in breaking the street lights and the porch light, how long would it be before the thing found a way to cut power to the house? No, better to find a weakness now than fight in the relatively cramped spaces inside where the shadow had a far greater advantage.

There was movement behind me. Good, the women retreated into the house, though they left the front door open to give me what light the house could still provide.

The shadow threw a rock at me, but I was too fast, and the rock sailed past. My gut told me the shadow might be off-balance from the throw, so I rolled into a *bananeira*, or handstand, which I was pretty sure the shadow wouldn't expect unless it had studied capoeira. Then, using the momentum from my last move, I aimed an *escorpião* (scorpion kick) at where the shadow's head should be. The sole of my foot definitely hit something solid, and the thing made a noise that sounded like a squeal, much higher pitched than I would have visualized. It also fell backward, giving me an opening.

The shadow wasn't well positioned to attack, so I ran in its direction rather than using an *aú*, or low-to-the ground cartwheel, which I might have needed to evade a blow. By the time I reached it, the shadow was standing again, so I hit it in the face with an *asfixiante*, a hard punch that drew another high-pitched sound from it and pushed it backward, though I could tell it was still conscious.

I also noticed it was armed. There was definitely some kind of blade clutched in its right hand, though whatever the weapon was made from was as dark as the shadow holding it and barely visible.

Most capoeira kicks and punches target the head, torso, or legs. Right now a kick to the weapon hand might have been more useful, but a good *banda* swept the thing's legs out from under it and caused it to land on the lawn with a thud. The thing definitely had a physical presence.

Once it was down, I stomped on its hand in a very un-capoeira way. It screamed, but it kept its grip on the weapon. I threw myself on top of it. Yeah, that was risky. I wasn't sure what its physical form was, but when I landed on it (with a satisfying thunk and another squeal from the thing), it felt human enough. In fact, it felt...female. I wasn't the most experienced guy in the world, but I recognized breasts when I landed on them. I had a twinge of guilt over fighting with a woman, but it...she...was trying to kill me.

I had sacrificed any possibility of evasion to pin her, but I was bigger and heavier than she was. Her struggles didn't come close to freeing her. I didn't give her enough space to knee me in the groin, and I grabbed her hands to prevent punching or scratching. My grip on her weapon hand was particularly strong to keep her from striking at me with it. As soon as I overcame my aversion to knocking her out with a good, old-fashioned head butt, the fight would be over.

Then the whole area lit up like noon. The shadow gave a satisfying scream, but I was momentarily blinded. In the second it took my eyes to adjust, she head butted me somehow, though I wouldn't have thought she could from her position.

Caught by surprise, I loosened my grip just a little, and she heaved beneath me with frenzied energy, creating more space between us, and then kneed me in the groin.

My brain stalled for a second as red pain surged through me, and she broke free. I was at a complete disadvantage now, and she might have stabbed me. Instead, probably from fear of the light, she ran like hell.

My eyes had adjusted enough to make out a deceptively small but definitely feminine body in a loose-fitting black outfit running at Olympic speeds into the shadows. I might have chased her, but my throbbing groin precluded that, and, in seconds, she vanished. I glimpsed light hair, probably blond, but I had no idea what her face looked like, not that I would ever need to. She would never come at me in a place with enough ambient light for me to see her face anyway.

"Are you all right?" Mom asked, bending over me, concern clear in her voice and face. In her hand she clutched the heavy-duty flashlight that she had probably thought would be helpful. It would have been, too—if I hadn't already won.

Sure, I'm fine. I'm just writhing here clutching my crotch for the fun of it!

"I'll be OK," I managed, "but we better get inside. Whoever or whatever that was may be back." I let her help me up, and then I hobbled toward the door with her fussing along behind.

Better the devil you know…

Chapter 4: Interlude (Umbra)

The Praeceptor didn't strike me, though she could have. She didn't need to, though; her words were weapons enough.

"You failed, Umbra. I sent you out against someone who isn't even considered an adult by the standards of his society, and he defeated you. If not for luck, he would have captured you, and the consequences of that for the Populus Umbrae would have been unimaginable."

"I would never have revealed anything," I said quietly.

"You would have revealed it all in time," the Praeceptor said sadly. "The humans now know you are vulnerable to light. They would have locked you away in a place with no shadows, and therefore no escape. Then they would have tortured you until you revealed everything."

"Umbra," she continued almost gently. "You were such a promising student. How could you allow your target to get the better of you like that?"

"His abilities are greater than we thought—"

"Do you blame me, then, for your failure?" asked the Praeceptor, a dangerous edge in her tone.

"The error was mine, Praeceptor. I knew he was fast, but I could not figure out his fighting style. I have never seen it before. I will not make the same mistake again."

"How comes it that there even was a fight? It is better always to approach by stealth and kill before your presence is even suspected."

"Such was my intent," I tried to explain, "but he knew I was there somehow, and even in the darkness, he could see me."

There was a long, torturous silence, and I was sure the Praeceptor would criticize me for trying to shift blame again. Instead, she said, "If what you say is true, then we may have misjudged this human. We suspected he belonged to a fey bloodline because of his speed, but perhaps he inherited other abilities that our research should have been thorough enough to uncover. A dominus would never forgive such an omission on a real mission.

"Based on this new information," she continued, "I may be able to convince the other praeceptors that a second trial is warranted before making the decision that you are unnecessary. Knowing more about him now, do you think you could defeat him?"

"I am sure I could," I said quickly, knowing that was the only answer that would keep me alive. Inside, I was not so confident. The target had surprised me, and perhaps he would again. If our original assessment of him was wrong, he could still have tricks about which we knew nothing. I would also need to study the way he fought, and I had no idea whether I would be allowed the time to complete such a study.

"That is well," said the Praeceptor. "Prepare yourself, and I shall speak to my colleagues." She did not say good-bye; she never did. I sensed, however, that she was gone.

The questions I wondered about most remained unanswered. I did not dare ask them.

As far back as I could remember, I had been taught that light would burn me. It stripped away my cloaking shadow and made it difficult to see, but I felt no burning, and my skin remained unmarked. I knew I was not like my fellow *sicarii*, but I had no idea how much difference there was between me and them. Perhaps the fact that light didn't destroy me was the reason I had been chosen, but then why not simply tell me that?

The other question would have been even harder to ask.

Everyone here was cold to the touch…everyone except me. When the human male was on top of me, when his hands gripped mine, I felt his body heat. It was like mine.

No one here sweat…except me. When the human male pressed against me, I felt sweat on him…again, just as he would have felt on me.

I had studied humans somewhat, mostly in terms of how to kill them as needed, or how to hurt them in a fight if I had to fight one. In all these years, though, no one had ever told me they had the same physical peculiarities I did. Even his face, his hair, the general structure of his body, with a few obvious differences, resembled mine far more than did the featureless praeceptors and *sicarii* around me.

I tried to ready myself for another effort to kill the human, but that one question haunted me.

Was I human myself?

Chapter 5: Dancing with Shadows (Lucas)

An aspirin and a couple of ice packs later, I was more or less good to go…well, except for the whole not knowing whom to trust thing.

The mystery woman though, made a good point as the three of us sat around the kitchen table. "Lucas," she said, "you must have known for some time that you aren't an ordinary boy, and your mother and I both saw you move faster than humanly possible. You've also admitted to being chased by a shadow that turned out to be a girl. If you can accept that, why would you think it so strange for me to be an Encantado?"

She had me there. I had known I was different ever since puberty, and having Encantado genes could explain a lot. However, there were still holes in her story.

"Why haven't I heard any of this before?" I leaned forward.

The mystery woman sighed. "For many reasons, some of them too complex to explain fully now. Your mother may have been right in thinking that knowing would place a burden on you."

"More of a burden than knowing I could do things others couldn't but having no idea why?" I asked—though really, if my concern was being a freak, I'm not sure knowing I descended from what amounted to magical weredolphins would have helped a whole lot.

"I'm truly sorry," Mom said, sounding sincere. "This kind of power often skips several generations. I myself have almost none, and there was every reason to think you'd lead a normal life and never need to know about your background."

That didn't make me much happier, but I had to agree it made sense. "You said reasons, plural," I reminded the mystery woman.

"Once the supernatural…species, I suppose you would call them, mingled much more freely with humans, and the Encantado continued to have love affairs with them into early modern times." Mom cleared her throat at that.

Yeah, great, so I'm not just descended from weredolphins, but from horny weredolphins!

"But," I prompted, "something changed."

The mystery woman nodded. "Over the centuries, it became harder and harder to visit your world, and some lost the privilege completely—usually those who allowed themselves to be worshiped as gods.

My people assumed that they had better watch out, or they too might find themselves confined to the Encante. We still visit occasionally, but very discreetly, and we never reveal ourselves to mortals. I can be honest with you only because you are of my blood and need my help. Had you not been in peril, I would have been...discouraged, let us say, even from visiting, much as I longed to. That is why you know me only by letter and old faded photographs. I used to visit your mother much more often, and I was punished for taking too much of a risk."

"I guess that makes as much sense as anything else that's happened today," I admitted. "It's just a lot to take in all at once."

"And neither one of us wants to rush you," said—uh, might as well provisionally think of her as *Bisavó*. "Unfortunately, we may not have much time. The *pessoas da sombra* will not wait long to come after you again."

"By the way," Mom interrupted, "that was very brave of you to face that shadow...and very foolish. What would *Mestre* Ribeiro say about confronting an opponent whose capabilities are not known to you?"

"I didn't have much choice, now did I?" I asked. "An unknown opponent could just as easily have struck while we were inside the house. None of us knew then how light sensitive she was."

"Which is why I will tell you all I know," *Bisavó* said, "though it is not as much as I wish I could tell, and part of it was proved wrong tonight.

"Most early cultures regarded a person's shadow as something supernatural, but as far as anyone knows, this particular group of shadows originated in ancient Greece. Some Greeks believed it was possible to sacrifice one's shadow to Zeus. Others thought that if worshipers entered the temple of Zeus Lycaeus, their shadows would be taken from them."

"Surely neither of those things is true!" I protested.

"Probably not," *Bisavó* conceded, "but it does seem to be true that at a person's death, at least in ancient Greece and Rome, his or her shadow went to a place called *Terra Umbrae*, the Land of the Shadows, in the underworld."

"What for?" I asked impatiently.

"No one knows," she admitted. "All we know is that over centuries, a great many shadows accumulated in some supernatural realm.

They may not have had thought processes in the beginning; no one knows. However, they seem to have developed thoughts over time. Maybe evil was inherent in their natures, or maybe they sucked it in from the air in the underworld, and they developed a society whose sole purpose was to train assassins."

With an audience like my great-grandmother and my mother, I couldn't use the expletives I wanted to. "This sounds like a fairy tale," was all I could politely get out on the spur of the moment.

"I only wish it was," *Bisavó* said. "Think about it though, and you will see how logical it is. Somehow, the *pessoas da sombra* found a…hole; yes, a hole…that led into your world. They moved faster than humans—other than people like you, anyway—and in darkness they could strike unseen—again, except against people like you. I gather you were late tonight because you encountered your assassin earlier. You must have realized she was there, yes?"

I nodded impatiently, now hungry for every detail she could give me.

"What evil being would not pay well for a fast, undetectable killer? In many realms, their services became highly demanded. Oh, escaping undetected after the deed was done is also something they are famous for. Apparently, they can travel from one shadow to another without passing through the space in between. They can also travel through shadow back to the Land of Shadows. The Encantado can do much the same with water."

I had a light bulb moment. "That's how she kept getting in front of me when I tried to run home!"

"Indeed, they are difficult to elude at night," *Bisavó* agreed. "But even during daylight, if one really wanted to follow you, it could jump from one shadow to another. Somehow, probably by magic, as long as they are in shadow, they can see an area near the shadow, regardless of how well-lit it is. Only if they are actually in the light does it blind them."

"Why would someone want to kill me, though?" I asked. "What have I ever done to anyone that was so bad?"

"Nothing I know of," *Bisavó* replied. "Carolina, is there anything?"

"No, Lucas is a good boy," Mom replied firmly. "He's never hurt anyone."

"Then I would guess it's a training exercise."

"Shadows need to be trained?" I asked, having a hard time visualizing that kind of school. "Actually, something else doesn't make sense. What I fought tonight didn't seem like just a shadow; she seemed human."

"And that, *Bisneto*, is the most frightening part," *Bisavó* replied. "She was afraid of the light, but she wasn't a shadow, or light would have done more than just scare her off. It may be that she actually is human."

"You mean...like a changeling?" Mom asked, eyes wide.

"I'm afraid so," *Bisavó* said. "Consider this from the point of view of the *pessoas da sombra.* Having trained humans as assassins would be a great step forward for them. The *sombras* are fast, but it takes effort for them to become solid enough to strike a physical blow, and enough direct light will drive them out of your world. They could teach human agents to operate in full daylight, though the girl we just saw hasn't been prepared this way yet. Quite a training strategy if they could get it to work, though. Totally brilliant...and totally evil!"

This conversation was becoming like English class without *Spark Notes*. "You mean, she's like those kids in fairy tales who, uh, get kidnapped and taken to live with the fairies?"

Bisavó nodded. "Though some of the children taken by faeries actually ended up happy. It's hard to imagine how a human child could ever be happy in the Land of the Shadows."

"Do you think she realizes she's human?" Mom asked.

"She knows human anatomy pretty well," I said ruefully.

"Judging by the way she reacted to light, I doubt it," *Bisavó* replied, though she seemed uncertain.

"Well, whether she knows she is or not, is she vulnerable to anything humans are?" I asked. "She certainly seemed to react to a punch or kick the way a human would."

Bisavó considered a moment. "She clearly has the ability to use shadow magic, and she can see in the dark. These signs suggest the *sombras* have...made changes in her. However, your combat experience suggests she is still basically human."

"Then it should be relatively easy to capture her and end this," I said, smiling for the first time in hours.

"Ah, *Bisneto*, if only it were that easy. How would you propose to keep her captive? Your house is not exactly a prison, and even if it were, she needs only one shadow to travel back to the Land of the Shadows. Almost certainly, we will have to kill her."

"I'm not killing her!" I said, hardly able to believe what I was hearing. "If you're right, she's been brought up and brainwashed by these…shadows. She still has parents somewhere who don't know what happened to her. We can reunite—"

"Stop!" *Bisavó* commanded. "She was probably kidnapped as an infant. She doesn't know her parents, and I doubt she can adapt to living in human society again. Even if she could, could she overcome her training? She's a trained killer, not some poor, misguided girl you can save. She might pretend to be grateful to be rescued, only to come after you later."

"Still, killing someone…Mom?" I turned in her direction.

She seemed to be studying the table top with great interest and did not meet my eyes.

"*Mãe*? Do you want your son to be a killer?"

"I want you to be alive!" she snapped at me with unexpected ferocity. "If the only way to keep you alive is to kill her, I'll kill her myself!" Finally she looked in my direction, her eyes filled with tears.

"There has to be another way!" I insisted. "Please, *Bisavó*! Please think of something else!"

Bisavó looked both pleased and surprised by my acknowledgment of her, but she wasn't thrilled with my tone. "Lucas, don't be selfish! Even if we could keep you safe from her, she's bound to kill someone else eventually. That's what the *sombras* took her for in the first place. Suppose, though, that a miracle happened, and she decided she wanted to rejoin human society? Do you think they would leave her alone so she could start over here? No, *Bisneto*, they would kill her anyway."

I pushed my chair back so hard I probably scraped the linoleum, but I didn't care. "Is this how it works in your world, *Bisavó*? Do people have to kill all the time in the Encante?

"We are lovers, not fighters," replied *Bisavó*, watching me intently. "There is no violence to speak of. Wait! That gives me an idea."

"Well?" I said after a long pause. "What's the idea?"

"You aren't going to like it, but it will avoid killing the girl, if that is truly what you wish."

"It is," I agreed.

"Since you are part Encantado, there is nothing stopping you from coming back with me to the Encante. It's an underwater realm, but I can make it possible for you to breathe there. Given how difficult it is for Encantado women to seek human lovers anymore, you will be…very popular."

"Gabriela!" Mom said, clearly shocked. "In our society Lucas isn't even of age. I want him alive, but I don't want him to become the…boy toy for your…your bridge club."

"Don't be silly!" *Bisavó* replied. "We don't play bridge in the Encante."

I had only one thought at this point: *sign me up!*

Miraculously…and unfortunately, my mind kept working.

"How long would I stay?" I asked, visualizing the whole idea as if it were a really great vacation plan.

"You would have to stay your whole life," *Bisavó* said gently. "A *sombra* assassin never gives up until the job is completed. I can keep you safe there, but there's no way to keep you safe here.

"In fact," she continued, "As I think about it, even if she dies, the *sombras* will just send someone else. The organization is as single-minded as the individuals. We should probably take you to the Encante this very night."

"You mean I won't ever see him again?" asked Mom, shocked. Clearly, she had not anticipated this turn of events any more than I had.

"We might be able to arrange an occasional quick visit during the daytime," *Bisavó* said. "But even that's risky now that they are using humans. Of course, you could come along yourself, Carolina, as you also are part Encantado."

Mom took less than fifteen seconds to digest that. "And Paulo?"

"These days, the rules are strict about someone who is fully human coming to the Encante. Only if he is a lover of a full Encantado would such a thing even be considered," *Bisavó* replied.

"But…but…he's my husband!" Mom protested.

"We can make the argument," *Bisavó* said, with less sorrow than I thought appropriate, "but there is no guarantee anyone will listen."

"I'm not going anywhere without my parents…both my parents," I said. I didn't add that I didn't really want to leave all my friends, dance and capoeira behind either. One thing at a time.

"I cannot keep you safe here!" *Bisavó* snapped. "It simply cannot be done."

"Then I'll have to keep myself safe," I said. "I'll be like the dude in *Darkness Falls* who doesn't go out at night, has a house in which every corner is lit, and carries flashlights with him all the time, just in case."

"And that will work precisely as long as it takes the *sombras* to figure out what you are doing. Then they'll train a human to come after you in broad daylight, and you'll be done." *Bisavó* sounded tired now more than angry.

"You've seen me fight," I insisted, "and I'll just get better from here. I can see the shadow assassins coming, and I can move faster than any of the human ones."

"I don't want this either," Mom said, "but Lucas, to have to watch your back every day for the rest of your life? Would that even be a life?"

"Life or not, it's mine!" I almost shouted. "I will do with it what I want—and I want to stay here!"

Bisavó looked amazed. "Lucas, I thought you were just part Encantado; I didn't realize you were part mule!"

I was ready to storm off dramatically, go straight up the stairs and slam my bedroom door—not perhaps the most mature exit, but dramatic enough to make my point—when the lights went out.

Chapter 6: Power Failure (Lucas)

"Is this a spell?" Mom whispered.

Bisavó frowned. "Magic doesn't generally work directly against technology...but where are your circuit breakers?"

"Outside," said Mom, "but the box is locked."

"I'd say our assassin can also pick locks or found a way to break one," said *Bisavó*. "Either way, we have no choice but to fight now. There's no nearby body of water I can use to take Lucas to the Encante."

If capoeira had taught me anything, it was focus, and the lights going out caused me to quickly shuffle through different scenarios. "Upstairs bedrooms now!" I ordered. "We can lock ourselves in, and the only way to come at us is through the one door."

"What about—" Mom began.

A floorboard creaked in the living room. Had the assassin entered the now darkened house? If so, she really could travel from shadow to shadow. We didn't have time to get upstairs. She could be upon us any second.

"Scratch that; stay right here!" I said quickly, although I wasn't confident they would do what I told them. I grabbed the high-powered flashlight Mom had used earlier. Then I raced into the living room, rapidly swinging it back and forth. The beam hit nothing at standing height, which made me suspect the assassin had borrowed some capoeira maneuvers and was staying close to the ground. Before I adjusted my angle, a rock hit the flashlight with such force that it shattered the plastic lens, as well as the bulb. She had quite a throwing arm, not to mention deadly accurate aim! Under other circumstances, I would have admired that performance, but right now, I wondered how I'd survive.

She was willing to kill. I wasn't. She could see in the dark. I couldn't. I did know capoeira, but capoeira tactics rely on being able to see an opponent.

But I suddenly realized I *could* see her, just as I could when she followed me on the street, except now I could perceive the real her—her human body, or at least the outline of it, not just its shadowy cocoon. From the way she was approaching, I guessed she hadn't yet realized I knew where she was.

I started an *aú*, and when, as I expected, she lunged at me, I shifted to *aú batido*, a broken cartwheel in which I stopped at the handstand and hit her with a perfectly executed *martelo*. The L-kick to the head caused her to lose her balance and fall forward instead of finishing her lunge. She was moving at the wrong angle for me to take her down with a sweeping kick. Instead, I used my speed to get in front of her, and then came up in an *escorumelo*, a head butt from below that struck her beneath the chin hard enough to rattle her teeth and jerk her head back. She staggered backward, probably in pain, and almost certainly disoriented. I just needed to take her down and subdue her—being careful not to repeat my mistake from last time.

The whine of a siren and the flashing lights of the police cruiser interrupted my thought, giving my supposedly helpless opponent the chance to throw her weapon at me. Normally, someone reeling backward like that would have been hard-pressed to aim, so her training must have been incredibly effective. The weapon scratched me on the way past, and the distraction gave her enough time to disappear back to wherever she came from.

"Lucas?" my mom called uncertainly from the kitchen.

"I'm OK, and she's gone," I shouted back, trying to get the message across without giving the nearby police too much of an earful if any of them happened to be standing near the house.

Mom and *Bisavó* ran from the kitchen, and Mom hugged me a lot harder than seemed necessary.

Someone knocked on the front door. "Paulo? Lucas? Carolina? Are you guys all right?" the familiar voice of Officer Sullivan said.

"Answer it, Carolina," ordered *Bisavó*, taking her turn to hug me.

Mom opened the door. My father's worried-looking friend stood on the porch with his trusty police issue flashlight. He was careful not to blind Mom with the light, but it provided a little glow that was welcome—though the living room was still too full of shadows for my taste.

"Carolina," he said, "your porch light is broken…and it looks as if your power is out."

"It just went out." Mom made a show of looking over his shoulders at the dark street beyond. "It looks like some of the streetlights are out too."

"All of them on this block, actually." Sullivan scratched his head. "But not because they lost power. Every single one is broken."

"Kids, I think." Mom was apparently a much better liar than I had ever suspected. "I heard some pretty high voices outside."

"One of the neighbors called in earlier and reported some kind of fight on your lawn." Sullivan paused expectantly.

"We heard something also. Lucas was going to go out and investigate when the power went out. Must have been the same kids, don't you think?"

"Probably," Sullivan conceded. "It was dark, so the person who called in didn't really see much. Any idea who the kids were?"

"I wish I could help," Mom said, "but we didn't see much, either. I wouldn't let Lucas go outside and look without having a better idea what was happening."

"Well, it wouldn't have been a good idea anyway," Sullivan observed, "considering his condition, I mean."

I was standing behind Mom, so even if it had been lighter, I wouldn't have been able to tell what her expression was like, but evidently it was blank or surprised, because Sullivan continued, "The twisted ankle. He really should be staying off of it."

It's too bad Sullivan was good at his job. I sometimes wondered why he wasn't located somewhere with a larger, better-paying force…and tonight I wished that especially.

"Oh, I forgot, because it seems better already," Mom said lamely. Apparently she wasn't such a good liar after all. "I think Lucas was just mistaken about it being twisted."

Sullivan frowned. "I'm surprised someone like Lucas would make a mistake like that, what with dance and capoeira and all. He knows his body pretty well, doesn't he?" There was a long silence.

Mom was sinking fast.

"I'm afraid I underplayed the pain a little, Officer," I said, hobbling over to the door. "Didn't want her to worry. I'll see the doc about it tomorrow."

Sullivan smiled and seemed to buy it.Then he looked at my arm. "Lucas, you're bleeding." He pointed at my wound with the flashlight.

Damn! I'd forgotten the assassin nicked me. There was a little blood on my right bicep.

"Blood?" asked *Bisavó*, sounding panicked.

"Who's that?" asked Sullivan, raising the flashlight a little.

"Oh, my mother is visiting from Brazil," Mom replied.

Sullivan looked into the darkness, raised the flashlight a bit and seemed about to introduce himself, when a blood-curdling shriek captured our attention.

"I'll be back in a minute." He hurried off in the direction of the scream. "Stay inside!" he called back to us over his shoulder as he vanished into the darkness.

"Who's screaming?" I asked, visualizing shadow assassins popping up all over town.

I jumped a little when *Bisavó* grabbed my arm with surprising strength. "How did you cut yourself, Lucas?" she demanded.

The scream seemed higher priority to me, but she sounded so upset I answered her. "The assassin threw her…weapon at me."

"No!" she wailed, making my skin crawl. "No!"

"Gabriela, what is it?" Mom was obviously as creeped out as I was.

"The shadow blades…" she started, sounding as if she was crying. "They…they…are like poison to any living thing. One scratch is fatal."

"I'll call nine-one-one," said Mom, fumbling for the phone.

"And tell them what?" asked *Bisavó*, her voice still tearful. "That your son has deadly shadow magic in his blood? His hurt is supernatural. Doctors can do nothing. Who is the local *curandera*?"

There was far too long a pause. "I don't know of any. There may be one in Merced…"

"He'll die before we reach Merced," *Bisavó* insisted. "Think, Carolina! Think! We have to find a closer one."

"I don't know of any!" Mom almost shouted in frustration.

"I'm OK," I said quietly. "I feel fine."

That caused a momentary pause in *Bisavó's* plunge toward hysteria. "You should already be feeling something. Maybe the blood means you got injured some other way. We need light in here."

"I'll reset the breakers," said Mom.

"But the screaming—" I started. Someone was reaching epic levels of terror, and I didn't want Mom to go outside until we knew what was happening.

"I created the screaming," said *Bisavó*. "It was to get the police to worry about something besides your full-of-holes story. Carolina, the breakers, now!"

Mom fumbled back through the kitchen and toward the back door.

Bisavó still gripped my arm hard enough to cut off circulation. "You can let go now," I said gently.

"Pray; pray the blood is from something else." Her grip loosened a little. She seemed determined to hold on to me, as if she could keep me from dying that way.

Dying? She must be wrong about that; I still felt fine. Her certainty was a little frightening though. People my age did sometimes die, obviously, but it's one thing to know that intellectually. It's completely different to accept it emotionally.

In a couple minutes the lights came on, and none too soon. *Bisavó's* hands trembled on my arm, and that didn't help my state of mind. Nor did the incessant screaming outside, though at least now I knew it wasn't real.

Bisavó looked at the small cut on my arm, seemed uncertain, and frantically searched of the room.

"What—" I started.

"The blade!" she said. "I have to find the blade!"

Mom returned and helped. I just kind of stood there like an idiot. My brain was playing catch-up. Everything I thought I knew about the world was dissolving right in front of me, and I wasn't yet sure what would replace it. Mostly I just wished I could go back to this morning and relive the day with no shadow assassins in it.

"Is that it?" asked Mom.

"Yes, but don't touch it!" *Bisavó* cautioned. She bent over something in the corner, and I walked over to see.

I blinked a couple of times. There was something, but it was hard to see in the light. It looked like a random piece of shadow somehow sharpened to a point. Something else glistened along its edge.

"Blood! It has blood on it!" *Bisavó* was back into full-on panic mode.

"I feel fine!" I protested again, but neither Mom nor *Bisavó* were paying any attention to me.

"Can't you do something?" asked Mom.

Bisavó had started crying again. "We Encantado don't have healing powers!"

"I'm fine," I said more loudly. Still no response.

"Could we just...cut off the poisoned part?" asked Mom.

"The shadow poison has attached itself to his life-force," managed *Bisavó*, between sobs. "Even cutting off the arm would not save him now."

Cutting off the arm?

"I'm fine!" I almost shouted. "If some poison were in me, shouldn't I feel something?"

Bisavó looked stunned for a second. Then, after wiping her tears, she looked at my arm again.

"There is something there, Lucas," she said, "but it is strange that you feel nothing. I have heard of people dying in less time than this."

"Doesn't that mean I'm fine?" I asked.

"This minute, yes. At any moment, however, the poison could start to work."

"You said yourself people usually die right away!" I said accusingly. She almost sounded as if she were making up rules as she went along. Maybe she didn't really know what she was talking about.

"I can sense foul magic on the blade, and I can sense the same magic in your arm. Why it hasn't started to work yet...I'm not sure. That doesn't mean the danger isn't real, *Bisneto*; it just means we might have more time than I thought. Perhaps this blade's magic was designed for a human, and since, you have some Encantado ancestry, the power will take a little longer to manifest itself."

I was tempted to answer that explanation with expletives. *Bisavó* seemed to be scaring us all for nothing. I had been scratched by the deadly blade, but I was fine. Why couldn't that satisfy her?

"What do we do now?" asked Mom. "We might have time to find a *curandera*..."

"Since we do seem to have more time than I thought, I have a better way to use it than hunting for someone who may or may not be powerful enough to do the job," said *Bisavó*. "I am owed a rather large favor by one of the best healers I know of. Given a few minutes, she may be able to reach Lucas or bring Lucas to her, and she will be able to heal him; I know she will!"

Much to my surprise, *Bisavó* produced a cell phone from her purse. I don't know what I expected. Telepathy maybe or smoke signals or pretty much anything less modern.

Bisavó managed a weak smile for me. "Modern technology has its uses. This healer is a great distance away, but I have a...what would be your term? Hotline number? Yes, I have a hotline number for her."

She dialed and got an answer almost immediately. "This is Gabriela Golfinho...yes, of the Encantado. Coventina gave me this number if ever I needed healing. No, it is not for me; my *Bisneto* has been scratched by a blade of the *pessoas da sombra*...uh, yes, you would call them *Populus Umbrae*. Yes, he's alive, or I wouldn't be calling. Yes, I'm sure he's wounded. Listen, I have no idea how long he has. I need help, not questions. Can't you at least send somebody to investigate? Yes, we are in...Lucas, what's the name of this hole-in-the-wall town again?"

Gee, how do you really feel about it?

"Madisonville," I said quickly.

"Yes, Madisonville, California," she told whoever was on the other end of the line. "It's a fairly new place, just a little east of Merced." Then there was a long pause. "What? Santa Brígida? Where's that? Santa Barbara? That's...how long a drive is that?"

"Almost five hours," I said. "Why?"

"It's a five-hour drive!" she exclaimed into the phone. "Isn't there anyone closer? I don't know how long he has. Don't you understand? Oh, all right! Call me back, but make it quick!"

I sensed this was one of those times when *Bisavó* would rather have been on a landline, if only for the satisfaction of slamming down the receiver.

"Aren't they being cooperative?" Mom asked apprehen-sively.

Bisavó sighed. "I think the fellow I was talking to is doing what he can. I'm just frustrated by the limitations of magical travel."

"What do you mean?" I asked. "Isn't it...well...magical?"

Bisavó managed a very small laugh. "Magic has its own rules...and those rules differ depending on the kind of magic. We of the Encantado can travel from the Encante to any large natural body of water, whether we've ever been there or not. The people I'm trying to get help from can travel by water too, but only fresh water, and they generally have to have visited the destination. They can also open a portal to Annwn, their world, and they can then open a portal from there to any place on Earth—but again, with the limitation that they have to have been there before. The man I talked to is scrambling to find someone who's visited this area before. If he can find someone, we could get help almost instantly. If not, well, the closest healers they have are in Santa Brígida, five hours away."

"Who are 'they'?" asked Mom, in a who-is-my-child's-life-depending-on kind of tone.

"The Order of Ladies of the Lake," replied *Bisavó*. "There aren't any better healers...at least, not accessible from this world."

"Wait, you mean like the Lady of the Lake in the King Arthur stories?" I asked skeptically.

"There was always more than one," said *Bisavó*. "Over the centuries, they have developed a huge organization, including a bureaucracy that handles the details when they need to work with mortals. That's why Coventina had a phone number to give me.

"Coventina's their leader," she continued in response to my questioning look. "A number of years ago, I rescued a couple of the Order's agents in Brazil, and Coventina herself, though she hardly ever leaves her headquarters these days, came in person to promise me assistance if ever I needed it."

"A phone number seems...an odd way to do business," observed Mom. "Why not give you some magical object as a way to contact them?"

"And so indeed she did," said *Bisavó* sadly. "It was stolen from me. I should have asked for another, but somehow I never got around to it, and now I have failed Lucas!" She looked as if she were going to cry again.

"First, I'm fine," I said quickly. "Second, you couldn't have foreseen this kind of situation. Third, I think I can speed this process up."

"You can?" *Bisavó* asked, looking at me with desperate hope.

"We know someone from the Order probably hasn't visited Hicksville, but I can think of two ways to get together with a healer faster than five hours. We could drive to Lake Yosemite, and you could transport us through that to any other body of water, right?" I asked.

"Lake Yosemite is the way I came here, and yes, from there I can go to any large natural body of water," agreed *Bisavó*.

"Great! You could transport us to Lake Cachuma. It's in the Santa Barbara area and reasonably close to Santa Brígida. Travel time shouldn't be more than one hour from here to the lakes and over to Santa Brígida."

"You've been there?" asked *Bisavó* hopefully.

"Not actually in Santa Brígida, but *Mestre* Ribeiro arranged for me to participate in some *rodas* in the Santa Barbara area. Come to think of it, one of the Santa Brígida guys was there, and he visited me up here. He does mixed martial arts, not capoeira, but he wanted to observe."

"What? You know someone from Santa Brígida?" asked *Bisavó*. She almost sounded accusing. "Why didn't you tell me?"

"I didn't realize it was important."

"Oh, was that the nice Persian boy?" asked Mom. "The one you invited to dinner a couple years back?"

"That's the one," I confirmed.

"He was here? In this very house?" asked *Bisavó* in mounting excitement.

"Yeah," I said, "but so what? He's not a healer, is he?"

"The Ladies of the Lake have techniques for linking with others. I think one of their healers can get here if she can link with this boy. What's his name?"

"Shar something. Oh, Shar Sassani I think." I said, hoping I had the name right.

Bisavó was on the phone almost instantly repeating the name to whoever was on the other end. Then she turned to me again.

"He wants to know if this location is secure."

I thought about our situation. The shadow assassin could rearm and come back, but if I understood the situation, nowhere with any shadow at all would be secure in that sense. I was more worried about Sullivan coming back than anything else. The screaming had subsided, so I assumed *Bisavó* had used it to lead him somewhere else, but, at some point, he was bound to pop up again, and I had no idea how long this would take.

"If we don't want to be interrupted, the back parking lot of the high school would be better. It's lit all night, so we don't have to worry about assassins, but it's not visible from the street. Shar's been at the school too. He was a guest speaker in Ms. Carson's world history class. People who know Persian history well are in pretty short supply in Madisonville."

Bisavó repeated everything I said, hung up, and turned to us with the biggest smile I had seen on her face. "It will take a few minutes, but they're sending us two of their best healers. This Shar will come along as well, and he and someone else they're sending will serve as bodyguards."

"Bodyguards?" asked Mom worriedly.

"The only reason we haven't had another visit from the *sombras* must be that they assume Lucas is as good as dead," replied *Bisavó*. "They could be watching though, and if Lucas is cured, it's possible he could be attacked, as could our guests if they get in the way."

"In that case, Mom, you should stay here," I said.

She started to protest, but *Bisavó* cut her off. "The boy is right. You should be safe here, but if you are at the school with Lucas and there is an attack, you would be the only one among us who couldn't defend yourself well. The assassin won't try to kill you, but things could get out of control—"

"I'm going!" Mom insisted.

"Yes…to sleep!" said *Bisavó*, waving her hand in Mom's general direction.

I felt something, a power I guessed, surge from *Bisavó* and strike Mom hard. She staggered and would have fallen if I hadn't grabbed her.

"What—" I started.

"We have no time to argue with her. She will sleep peacefully, just like your father, until I wake her."

"The street's pretty dark." I pointed out. "What if a robber decides now's a good time to break in?"

"There are police all over the place," *Bisavó* reminded me. "This isn't a night that would be especially attractive to robbers—at least on this block. Put your mother on the couch, and let's go," she finished, using what I imagined was her strongest don't-argue-with-me tone.

Bisavó had her work cut out for her to get us out though, as the disembodied screaming had worked a little too well. Police were herding anyone who popped out to see what was going on back into their houses. She could—and did—use her mastery of illusion to make us invisible and inaudible, but getting the car out of the garage was a whole other problem.

Preventing everyone from seeing a deep-impact metallic-blue Ford Explorer was apparently taxing to begin with, even in the dark, partly because of the headlights. Keeping people (who didn't see the vehicle) out of the way added an extra layer of complication. It took ten minutes to edge our way out of that block. Once we were back in an area that didn't look under siege, we became visible again and made normal progress, reaching the school in just a few minutes.

James Madison High School had the virtue of newness, though its design was uninspired and boxy; anyway, so said my dad, whose firm hadn't gotten the contract for it. I kind of had to agree, though. If you wanted a generic, institutional-looking environment, you could hardly have done better.

I drove up the back driveway, expecting to stop at the gate for the student parking lot—except it wasn't locked. The chain dangled from one side of the open gate, the unlocked padlock tucked neatly into the last link.

"Our guests?" asked *Bisavó*.

"Either that, or it's the tidiest break-in ever," I said.

Once we pulled around the curve in the driveway and into the lot itself, I could tell our suspicions were accurate. Our guests were already here...and they were not at all what I expected.

I had anticipated two women in long flowing white robes, Shar, and some thug. The term "bodyguard" was somehow linked in my head to hired muscle, and not necessarily muscle employed for entirely moral purposes.

Instead, what we got was one woman who was youngish, blond, and built like a *Playboy* model. (Yeah, I've taken my share of peeks at my dad's.) She was decidedly not in a long, flowing robe, but I managed to pry my eyes away from her to look more closely at the three guys with her.

Shar was only a year older than I was, and the other two looked about the same. Shar might not have been hired muscle, but he was definitely muscle, far more ripped even than the average high-school athlete. He looked as if he had worked out constantly since the last time I saw him—and he hadn't exactly been scrawny then.

I shouldn't have been able to tell so much about his physique, because he wore a loose-fitting outfit probably designed to allow as much freedom of movement as possible, sort of like capoeira clothing. The long-sleeved shirt looked almost like leather armor and matched his pants. Despite being loose, though, his clothing did show off his muscles, almost like...well, magic. I couldn't shake the feeling someone had designed the outfit for combat, leaving Shar free to move but showing his enemies exactly how much he had to work with.

That was crazy though...or was it?

The other two, one a little taller than Shar, were slightly less muscled but clearly athletic, and, like Shar, they wore leather-like outfits. All three had scabbards that hung from their belts with formidable-looking swords in them. I hadn't expected them to be armed. I was used to capoeira, which didn't involve weapons, but none of them were capoeiristas, so I shouldn't have been too surprised.

"Lucas!" said Shar happily when I got out of the car. "We were beginning to worry."

"It took a while to get out of our neighborhood," I explained. "The police got called in when our friendly neighborhood assassin started breaking things like streetlights."

"From what I've read of them, that sounds a little desperate." The woman stepped forward to shake hands. "I'm Viviane Florence, Order of the Ladies of the Lake."

"Ah, one of the healers!" said *Bisavó*, joining us. "You seem very young." Implicit in the last statement was the question, "Do you have enough experience to get the job done?"

"As an Encantado such as yourself would know quite well, looks can be deceiving," said Viviane, bowing slightly.

Bisavó, seemingly charmed, bowed back.

"But where is the other healer? I understood there would be two," said *Bisavó*, suspiciously.

"Allow me to introduce Taliesin Weaver, who is many things, healer among them," said Viviane. One of the guys stepped forward and extended a hand.

He had an elaborate design on the chest of his leather shirt, something with fire and musical instruments. He was about my height, with brown hair and eyes and was clearly about my age as well.

Bisavó was not impressed. "He's a boy!"

Embarrassed, I muttered, "He's my age, *Bisavó*, and you've been calling me a man all night."

"Well, he's certainly no Lady of the Lake!" *Bisavó* shot back.

"He was joined to the Lake by Coventina herself, after which he had to save a young man whose body was horribly mutilated," said

Viviane quietly. "That was the very first time Tal ever used his healing powers, but he successfully reconstructed the poor kid's body, a task that would have daunted many experienced healers."

"Tell her about the resurrection," suggested the tall guy.

"We don't know what caused that," said Taliesin, looking embarrassed by the whole thing.

"*Bisavó*, you were the one who insisted on urgency," I pointed out, trying to avoid having her humiliate me completely in front of people who had, after all, come at a moment's notice to help us out. "Is this really the time to ask for everyone's résumé?"

"You speak the truth," she said, though with obvious reluctance. It seemed as if no one except Coventina herself would have satisfied her.

"Let me introduce the rest of our party, then, and we'll get started," said Viviane smoothly. "Shahriyar Sassani Lucas already knows; he was our ride here, so to speak. He and Gordy Hayes will keep watch in the event that Tal and I are too preoccupied with the healing to defend ourselves."

Both Shar and Gordy nodded in acknowledgment. I noticed they, too, had designs on their chests; Shar had an ancient battle scene, and Gordy a lion. The whole thing seemed almost...I don't know...like superheroes, and it made me want to snicker, but I suppressed that impulse.

"More children," muttered *Bisavó*, but I was relieved to see that our guests seemed able to practice selective deafness and pretended they hadn't heard her.

"OK, let's see what we have here," said Taliesin in an almost medical way. Past the awkwardness created by *Bisavó*, he now seemed far more mature than his years. "Right arm?"

I nodded, and he put one hand on each side of the clotted little scratch.

"I think you guys probably came out for nothing," I said apologetically. "I'm fine." I felt the oddest sensation in my arm as he examined it. I assumed he was using magic of some kind, and I could feel him doing it.

"Well, buddy, we didn't come out for nothing." Taliesin frowned. "You've got some pretty major evil magic in your arm. I'm just as surprised as your great- grandmother that it didn't do anything right away. It looks as if it should have killed you in minutes. Nurse Florence?"

Viviane stepped over and did the same thing—and, again, my arm felt weird, as if I could sense her looking around in it.

She cringed visibly. "Terribly strong magic. Shadow assassin for sure, though I've only seen it once before."

"And you saved the victim?" asked *Bisavó.*

"No," said Viviane sadly. "By the time I reached him, he was already dead."

Taliesin touched my arm again. This time, I felt the presence of his magic more strongly. Either I was becoming more sensitive, or he was using much stronger magic.

"For lack of a better way to describe what's happening, the poison is thinking," he said at last. "It was expecting a human, and now it's trying to adapt."

"I am human!" I protested, realizing as soon as I said it that I really wasn't—not completely anyway.

"You are human, of course," agreed Taliesin, "but also more, right?"

Before I could answer, a little boy's voice asked, "Like me?"

"Khalid!" exclaimed Taliesin, not angry exactly, but definitely not happy either. "What are you doing here? Shar, didn't you check for him?"

Shar looked embarrassed. "We were in such a hurry, I forgot. It never does us any good anyway; he sneaks along somehow, no matter what."

"Khalid! Show yourself!" Taliesin ordered sternly.

A little boy, obviously Khalid, appeared out of nowhere. He also wore a leather-like outfit, and just like the others, it had an image across the chest, in this case of an ancient Middle Eastern city with a small figure flying over it. He carried what looked like a real long bow, except it was sized for him, and there was a quiver of arrows on his back. Something about him made me think of Cupid, Middle Eastern style.

"You weren't supposed to come," said Taliesin reprovingly.

"You might need my arrows," Khalid said quickly, "and we've been in way more dangerous places than this." Then, looking at me, he smiled and asked, "Are you part djinn too?"

"What, like a genie?" I asked, not sure what he had said.

"More or less," said Shar. "Khalid is a half djinn."

I couldn't help but gawk a little.

Taliesin leaned close to me and said quietly, "Did you think you were the only one? The only one with part supernatural ancestry, I mean."

"Until tonight I didn't know I had supernatural ancestry," I said. "I'm still trying to get used to the idea."

Taliesin studied my face for about half a minute. "Thought you were a freak, right?" he asked, even more quietly.

Though I had just met him, something made me want to trust him, and I nodded.

"I've been there," said Taliesin reassuringly. "But guess what? Neither one of us is a freak. Khalid isn't either."

Khalid had moved closer to join the conversation. "I'm fire-proof, I can move pretty fast, and I can jump pretty high. What can you do?"

God! This really is like a superhero comic book!

"I can move fast too," I said, smiling at Khalid. "Sometimes I see things before they happen."

"Which is how you avoided the assassin, I imagine," suggested Taliesin. "I was told you were part Encantado, though, and neither one of those are Encantado characteristics."

"Are you going to cure him, or do his family tree?" *Bisavó* interrupted loudly.

"*Bisavó*!" I said, embarrassed again.

"It's a legitimate question," said Taliesin smoothly. "Actually, knowing more about him may tell us what approach to take to cure him."

"In that case, I will tell you what I can," said *Bisavó* grudgingly. "I was permitted to have a long-term relationship with his great-grandfather because the man had xana blood."

"Ah!" said Viviane. "Yes, the xanas are the faeries in Galicia and Asturias. A fair number of their descendants traveled to the New World."

Suddenly, my right arm felt like an icicle was being jabbed into it.

Taliesin, who still had a hand on it, jumped. "The poison is on the move! Nurse Florence, now!"

Viviane moved back to me and put her hands on my arm. I felt her magic surge around the poison, walling it in.

"Everybody else, keep watch," Taliesin cautioned the guys. Then he focused on my arm, and I felt magic from both of them trying to enclose the poison. The poison fought back, and I felt as if the icicle was splintering into my bloodstream.

For the first time since the shadow had fled, I was afraid.

Chapter 7: Another Interlude (Umbra)

I could feel the Praeceptor's cold rage.

"You told me you could kill this one! You swore it!"

"He was wounded!" I protested. "I know he was!"

"Aye," admitted the Praeceptor, still angry. "Yet he is not dead. A dominus will never accept a mere wound as completion of the task, nor will we."

My cheeks were wet, though I did not understand why. "Am I without purpose now?"

"Nearly," said the Praeceptor, "but I have prevailed upon my colleagues to give you one more chance. It will not count as a completed trial, for they are insistent you be sent with help, but it will not count as a failure, either—at least if you succeed this time."

"More than one assassin?" I asked, puzzled. "How many?"

"As many as we can raise," replied the Praeceptor vaguely. "The imperator of the Populus Umbrae himself is determined that the target shall not escape, no matter what. The reputation of our whole society is at stake now."

"He is with others," said the Praeceptor, "and some of them are powerful. To atone for your earlier failure, you and those we send with you will ensure that not a one survives."

"You mean—" I began, though I do not know why that made me nervous.

"I mean take care of the original target first, but then kill anyone, human or otherwise, that you find with him. All must die!"

Chapter 8: Shadows of Armageddon (Lucas)

I heard a crash, and I knew without looking. One of the lights in the parking lot had been shattered.

"Shar!" yelled Taliesin, still keeping both hands firmly on my arm.

"On it!" said Shar. "Incoming…multiple incoming."

Another crash.

Now my whole arm was cold and numb. Taliesin and Viviane worked on it feverishly—I felt their power surging in my arm—but they were not doing enough. I felt weaker than I had been just a minute ago.

"I've never heard of shadow assassins working in groups," muttered Viviane.

"Our boy here gave the one such a hard time they had to send reinforcements," said Taliesin, giving me a pat on the shoulder.

Khalid jumped off the ground and hovered above us, like he was flying. I wondered if I were hallucinating.

"His armor helps him do it," said Taliesin, as if he could read my mind. Hell, for all I knew, maybe he was reading my mind.

Khalid fired an arrow. There was a bright explosion somewhere, followed by several wordless screams. I couldn't hear a thing, but I felt the seething emotions from the shadows.

Khalid fired a couple more, with equally satisfying results. Then I heard another crash.

"I want to help!" I said weakly.

"Appreciate the thought, but no," said Taliesin firmly. "It's taking everything we have just to slow the poison's progress. We can't risk losing contact with you, and if you exert, you'll spread the poison faster."

He made sense, but that didn't make me any happier. Some little kid I didn't even know was defending me, and I was doing nothing.

Shar and Gordy hung close, swords out, ready if the light failed us. I couldn't miss the emerald green glow from Shar's blade or the sunshiny glow from Gordy's.

Taliesin explained as he worked. "Shar's sword is essentially anti-magic. It prevents its wielder from being affected by hostile spells, and it breaks many spells if it hits them. Gordy's exudes sunlight, among other things. Either one should dispatch a shadow with a touch. Khalid's arrows, with their little radiant explosions, can probably take out more than one at a time."

"Stop the chatter, and focus on the healing!" demanded *Bisavó.*

"It's important to keep Lucas in the right mood. If he panics, the poison will act faster," Taliesin explained.

"I'm not going to panic!" I said, more from embarrassment than from offense.

Taliesin looked me in the eye. "Then you're a nut case. Any sane person would panic at least a little right now. Unfortunately, the poison really does feed on that reaction."

Two more crashes in rapid succession, and the parking lot looked much gloomier.

"Khalid! Can you get them far enough back that they can't throw things at the lights?" asked Taliesin.

"I'm trying!" Khalid said squeakily.

His arrow explosions had been pretty consistent, as had the shadow screams I felt, but it was as if one group was wiped out, and a new one took its place.

Another crash.

"We should charge them," Shar suggested loudly. "We'll cut right through them."

"You'll be scratched for sure!" I protested.

"Their dragon armor protects most of their bodies," muttered Taliesin.

"That leather stuff is…what…like dragon skin?"

"You can see that?" asked Taliesin. "Oh, of course you can! You could see the shadow assassin too, right?"

I nodded.

"Khalid can see the shadows, but the other guys can't. They'd be fighting blind. Shar, Gordy, stay close. Even with dragon armor, it's just too risky."

"We've only got three lights left," Shar pointed out. "If those go, they'll be all over us…all over you and your patient."

The cold reached my shoulder.

I heard another crash. My mind had started working more slowly, but I wondered if I was going to die here, out in my high school parking lot.

I wouldn't even be able to say good-bye to Gavin, to Mom and Dad.

"Nurse Florence, you think you can hold him for a minute?" asked Taliesin.

"Maybe, but only that, Tal. Without both of us, the poison will spread much faster."

"Hang in there, buddy," Taliesin said to me. Then he let go, jumped to one side, and drew his own sword, the blade of which burst into flames.

Shar and Gordy stepped aside. Taliesin moved toward the shadows, and then he used the sword like a flame thrower, spraying fire across a wide area. I suspected the light was more of a problem for the shadows than the heat. Either way, I felt lots of screams.

The cold reached into my chest. I coughed once or twice, hard, and Viviane looked alarmed.

"Tal, I need you right now!" she called.

Taliesin appeared at my side, with Shar and Gordy in tow, which surprised me. Shouldn't they be poised to defend us?

"Khalid! Keep firing in all directions until you're out of arrows!" yelled Taliesin, and several explosions lit up the night.

"Between my fire and Khalid's arrows, they'll stay back, at least until he stops shooting," said Taliesin, putting his hands back on me. "We have to cure Lucas before they try to advance again."

"You could drive them back another time if you needed to, right?" asked Gordy.

"I can't do that and hold back the poison," Taliesin pointed out.

"Could someone else do it?" I coughed again as the poison worked its way further into my right lung.

"I'm the only one who can work the swords that way," replied Taliesin. "They aren't really designed to…wait, Shar, get closer. Let's see if Zom can break the poison spell." Shar moved forward.

Taliesin took one hand off of my arm to put it on the sword hilt, and suddenly I was bathed in an emerald flood. The poison convulsed within me. For a second, I thought it was gone. However, as soon as the emerald light receded back to the sword, my arm went cold, and the poison advanced again.

"The spell is too powerful," said Taliesin, obviously frustrated. "The poison seems to be gone, but it reasserts itself almost immediately."

"Shar, give Zom to Lucas," Taliesin continued.

"I'm not trained in sword fighting," I said, trying to make my brain work.

"It's not to fight with; its power will keep the poison from doing anything while we pound the shadows with everything we've got," Taliesin explained.

I took the sword and felt immediately better. Evidently he knew what he was doing.

Then Taliesin started singing in a language I didn't understand, and I felt his power grow.

"What's he doing?" I whispered to Viviane.

"He can do magic without music," she explained, "but he's even stronger with it. We don't know exactly how many shadow assassins are left, but there could be a great number, so he's trying to generate as much power as he can."

Taliesin stopped singing long enough to yell, "Close your eyes!"

Just before I did, I saw Gordy hand Taliesin the sunlight sword. Even through my eyelids, I saw the blade flare like a supernova, and the screams of the shadows became deafening.

Suddenly there was nothing. Psychic silence all around us. Blessed silence. Taliesin had driven the shadows away.

Even *Bisavó* abandoned her skepticism at this point. "Wonderful, wonderful! You have destroyed them!"

"I wish it were that simple," said Taliesin.

"Creatures like shadows cannot be destroyed," added Viviane. "The kind of attack Tal used can banish them for a while, and the pain of it would make any ordinary creature think twice about attacking again, but, at least if the Order's records are correct, the Populus Umbrae will never give up on a target. They'll just keep coming back."

"We'll just have to kick their butts over and over until they get the message," said Gordy.

"What Nurse Florence is trying to tell us is that they'll never get that message," said Taliesin sadly. "We'll have to find a way to seal off the realm from which they originate, and that's a little above even my pay grade."

"From what you've told us, we're dealing with the shadows of ancient Greeks and Romans, right?" asked Shar. "Could the Olympians help?"

"The Olympians?" I felt a little overwhelmed again.

"Yeah, they're real too," said Gordy, "and we're on pretty friendly terms. One time Tal almost got very friendly with Aphrodite, if you know what I mean."

To my surprise, Taliesin, who had been so calm during a life-threatening situation, turned bright red, and *Bisavó* snickered, reminding me of the primary motive the Encantado had in visiting our world.

"To…to get back to…the point," stammered Taliesin, but he didn't get to finish.

"There's a girl over there, lying at the edge of the parking lot!" announced Khalid, who must have been scouting.

Shar and Gordy went over to retrieve her and came back in a couple of minutes.

She must have been the assassin girl. Even in the now-feeble light of the parking lot, I could tell her skin was pale, as if she lived underground. The contrast with her black outfit made her skin stand out, almost as if it were glowing.

For someone who had almost killed me earlier, she looked physically unimposing. She was relatively short and not obviously well-muscled. Magic must have done some of the heavy lifting.

Actually, I fought to not feel sympathy for her. She looked so helpless, lying unconscious in Shar's arms.

"That sunburst must have overwhelmed her so much it knocked her out," Taliesin said slowly. "She has to have spent almost her whole life in darkness."

"What do we do with her?" asked Gordy.

"Kill her!" suggested *Bisavó* emphatically.

"We don't kill people unless we have to," replied Taliesin calmly, "and she is no threat now."

"She will be when she wakes up!" argued *Bisavó*, clearly not about to let go of the subject. "And she isn't 'people' anyway."

"She was once," said Viviane quietly. "From the information Coventina gave us, it sounds as if she's a changeling; she was stolen from her parents and raised by the shadows to be a killer."

"I don't care how she came to be what she is!" replied *Bisavó* emphatically. "She tried to kill Lucas!"

"She will not try again; that much I can promise you," said Taliesin firmly. "We can keep her asleep easily enough. For the moment, she's more a logistical problem than a threat. We have more pressing issues, like finding a way to cure Lucas. He can't keep holding Shar's sword for the rest of his life."

"You're right," acknowledged *Bisavó*. "Curing Lucas is the most important thing right now."

"This isn't a good location anymore," said Taliesin. "Someone may have heard the lights breaking or seen that flare. Also, the shadows could attack again any time. They can probably track Lucas through the poison in his system, but I doubt they can do it while he holds Shar's sword. We should be able to move him without having them follow."

"Alcina's island?" asked Viviane.

Taliesin glanced at his watch. "It should be around nine in the morning there, so the shadows can't attack even if they figure out where Lucas is."

Viviane nodded and raised her arms, her forehead wrinkled in concentration. Slowly a silver whirlpool formed in the air in front of her, expanding until it was large enough to walk through.

"That's a portal," said Taliesin, noticing my worried expression. "This particular kind is Celtic magic. Nurse Florence and I can make one to connect to any of the other worlds we've been to, and, from there, to any point on earth we've been."

"Other worlds? You mean like Mars?" I asked, amazed.

Taliesin chuckled. "No, not planets. Worlds. Other planes of existence, or realms, if you prefer. The island we're going to is in another world, making it even harder for the shadows to track you."

Taliesin glanced in *Bisavó's* direction. "Ma'am, you're welcome to come with us, or we can use your memories to open a portal to the Encante if you'd rather."

"I am not leaving my *Bisneto* until he is well," *Bisavó* said firmly.

"In that case we'll all go straight to the island, but I'm going to go through and make sure it's safe first," said Taliesin. "I'll be back in a minute if all's well." He walked through the portal as if he were doing no more than walking through a doorway, and then vanished. In a surprisingly short time, he reappeared.

"It's all good!" he announced. "Ladies first!" He waved Nurse Florence and *Bisavó* through.

"Speaking of, what about the girl?" asked Shar.

"As I said, logistical problem," Taliesin said slowly. "We really shouldn't leave her here. As long as we keep her in the sun and keep her asleep, she shouldn't be a threat. Let's take her with us."

Shar nodded and carried the girl through, with Khalid and Gordy close behind him. Taliesin took me through last.

Even though I had been told what to expect, I was still jolted to suddenly be standing on a white, sandy beach with the early morning sun momentarily blinding me. When my eyes recovered, I noticed we were right at the shore, with waves almost reaching our feet, so Taliesin ushered us a little further inland. In the distance was what looked like a large medieval castle.

"What is this place?" I asked, continuing to look around.

"It used to be the headquarters for an Italian sorceress named Alcina," explained Taliesin. "We use it for special projects that are too risky to do at home, and it also makes a good place to hide if the need arises."

"What happened to Alcina?" I asked, feeling a little silly. Taliesin hadn't brought me here to give me a tour or a history lesson. Still, I had always been curious…

"I'll tell you later, Lucas. It's kind of a long story."

"Yeah, with us, pretty much everything is a long story." Gordy grinned. "At least the stories are interesting…most of the time."

"What are we going to do about healing Lucas?" Viviane asked pointedly.

"As I see it, if we can do it under any circumstances, we ought to be able to do it now," said Taliesin, looking in the general direction of the sun. "As long as Lucas holds the sword, the poison can't do anything, and the direct sunlight might make it weaker. We should be able to draw it out of him, and then I think the sun will do the rest."

They had me lie down on the sand, and then they went to work very quickly. Taliesin sang to amplify his power. The rhythm was so compelling, I wanted to get up and dance, but that would probably have looked silly, so I restrained myself. My legs felt nervous though, like they wanted to do something.

They put their hands on me again, and then I felt their power inside me, wrapping around the poison, enclosing it, trying to pull it free. It resisted. I could almost feel it digging in. They surrounded it, but they still couldn't draw it out.

"Damn!" said Taliesin. "I was sure we were going to get it out that time."

Bisavó tensed. "You're not giving up, are you?"

"Tal never gives up!" Khalid grinned widely.

"I'm not giving up at all," replied Taliesin, "but I do need to think a minute. Why is this poison so powerful?"

"At a guess, the Populus Umbrae had millenniums to experiment with it and very little else to do, at least in the beginning," replied Viviane.

"Well, we don't have millenniums to find an antidote," said Taliesin grimly. "In fact, we probably only have as long as daylight holds."

"I thought you said they couldn't track me as long as I held the sword," I said worriedly.

"I'm confident they can't," replied Taliesin. "They might, however, be able to track *her*," he continued, waving in the general direction of the assassin. "You know, our resident logistical problem. I didn't want to leave her in your town; she'd be dangerous to any normal person, even without her weapon. That was when I thought we could cure you on the first try. Now, though, I'm realizing that when it gets dark, the shadows might connect with her. At best, they'll retrieve her. At worst, they'll connect to this island through her, come here, and we'll have to fight that battle all over again, with the difference that they now have a better idea of our strategy."

"I said from the very beginning that we should kill her!" pointed out *Bisavó.*

I had trouble adjusting to the fact that my great-grandmother seemed so bloodthirsty.

"And you know, we might have to do just that," said Taliesin sadly, "but it's a last resort, understand?"

Bisavó glared at him but did not continue the argument.

"We're still nowhere with the poison, right?" asked Gordy, probably trying to change the subject.

"Yeah, we need to focus," agreed Taliesin. "So with a physical poison already in the bloodstream, what would a doctor do?"

"Introduce an antidote, if there was one," Viviane said almost instantly.

"Great!" Shar said grumpily. "We don't have one, or we would already have done that."

"Don't we?" asked Taliesin slowly. "What is the one thing the shadows can't take?"

"Light!" Khalid said eagerly.

"Yes, Khalid, exactly!" Taliesin agreed. "And Gordy, what does your sword radiate?"

"Light," he said, "but we can't exactly stick the blade into Lucas to get the light inside him."

"Of course not," said Taliesin, "but—"

"We might be able to capture some of the light magically and inject it into the affected area!" said Viviane.

"Could that be dangerous?" *Bisavó* asked suspiciously.

"I don't see how," Taliesin said, though he did seem to mull the idea over for a second. "The sword was blessed by Apollo, who has powers of healing as well as light. In fact, though its blade can be deadly in combat and brings disease with every wound, a mere tap of the blade administered to a friend can heal wounds. We have seen its power in action."

"Why not just tap Lucas with it, then?" *Bisavó* asked.

"Because the sword only heals physical injuries; it doesn't break spells," replied Taliesin.

Just to satisfy *Bisavó*, Taliesin had me hand let go of Shar's sword for just a second and tapped me with Gordy's. As Taliesin had predicted, Gordy's sword didn't cure the poison, and I had to grab Shar's sword back right away to prevent the poison from spreading again.

"You see?" asked Tal. "The light sword must not have been crafted with supernatural poisons in mind. That doesn't mean, though, that the poison can resist direct exposure to the blade's light. It's the best plan we have."

Apparently *Bisavó's* skepticism, allayed for a while by Taliesin's earlier display of magic, had come back in full force. "Why not take him to this Apollo, then? Surely the one who blessed the sword would know better what to do."

"We did think of that," said Taliesin patiently. "Unfortunately, Shar tells me his attempts to invoke the Olympians are hitting a blank wall. Usually that means they are in combat, or at least preparing for combat, and Olympus wouldn't be a safe place to take Lucas under those circumstances. It's also possible that the shadows, who, after all, live adjacent to the Greek underworld, have a direct route to the Olympian plane. Without research, we can't be sure."

"Then take Lucas to Coventina herself!" *Bisavó* insisted, her tone demanding and unyielding as steel. "I have done service for members of her Order, and she will help me."

"And she did help you; she sent us," said Taliesin, his voice calm but his eyes telling a different story. "That is no small thing, whatever you may think."

"Yet you cannot cure him!" *Bisavó* pointed out.

Taliesin's calm facade cracked at that. "We probably could cure him if you didn't keep interrupting!"

I was sure *Bisavó* was acting out of genuine feeling for me. That didn't prevent what she was doing from embarrassing the hell out of me.

"*Bisavó*, please!" I begged. "Let them try what Taliesin suggested. It can't hurt."

"He has never before done what he is suggesting!" *Bisavó* replied sternly. "Even he doesn't know it won't hurt you. Coventina, she will know what to do."

"Coventina has her own problems right now!" Taliesin snapped. "Not so long ago, headquarters was infiltrated by a powerful witch. The Lake itself might have been endangered, and certainly the Order's existence was. Nurse Florence and I stopped the witch from bringing through a hostile army.

"I doubt that whatever you did for Coventina quite compares," Taliesin continued, getting louder with each syllable. "I saved the whole damn Order—and even I wouldn't ask Coventina to take in someone marked by the shadows. Probably she wouldn't do it even for me. It would put the Order in jeopardy again. All it might take is Lucas's hand slipping off the sword for a second, and bam—the shadow army comes flooding in from some dark corner! Remember, headquarters is far underground and only has torchlight.

"You don't trust me? Fine! Take Lucas and go then. I'm guessing you can use the sea here to take him to the Encante. Let someone there heal him!"

By the time Taliesin finished, he was shaking. Before, he sounded far more adult than I would have expected. Now, though, he sounded more like a teenager throwing a tantrum. I was ashamed to have been the cause of making him come unhinged like that.

"How dare you!" *Bisavó* shouted. "My *Bisneto* is dying, and all you can think about is your own ego!"

I knew part of this was my fault, and, as embarrassed as the whole situation was making me, if I didn't man up now, things would only get worse. "*Bisavó*!" I said loudly. "Stop this…right now! You are being unfair to Taliesin and his friends."

"You…you would take their side…against your *Bisavó*?" she said, as if she couldn't believe such a thing was possible.

"Look, I know you care about me," I said, somewhat more calmly. "But I just met you today, same as them. And they're not bad people! They risked their lives for me. We owe them the courtesy of letting them try."

Khalid walked over to *Bisavó* and said, "Lady, Tal never fails at anything. You couldn't find anyone better."

Time froze for a moment. *Bisavó* seemed torn between hugging Khalid and slapping him. Glancing at Shar, I could see slapping him would have been a very, very bad idea, but I wasn't sure she picked up on that vibe.

Fortunately, she went with the hugging. "Child, you are so wise for your years." She looked up, her eyes wet with tears. "Maybe your friend is as well."

Taliesin walked over to her. "Ma'am, I'm sorry I lost my temper. I know you care about Lucas. The rest of us care too, and I didn't mean it when I told you to take him away. We are together in this until he is cured."

"I…am…sorry…" said *Bisavó*, as if each word cost her dearly. "What Lucas said was true; you have already risked your lives for him, without even knowing him. Try what you can."

Even having known her only a few hours, I could tell *Bisavó* was not completely convinced that Taliesin could do the job, but I figured she had the common sense to see he might be the best shot we had.

Unfortunately, Taliesin's plan to capture the light from Gordy's sword and somehow get it into the part of me where the poison lurked was harder than he thought. He was used to making these magic swords work like ray weapons or flame throwers, and Gordy told me he could even use his own to create a fire shield around himself and his allies during battle. However, he had been practicing that kind of thing for months.

What he had proposed, he had never tried, and he and Viviane spent a lot of time fussing with the sword without an immediate result. Shar, Gordy and Khalid made small talk with me, I suspect so I wouldn't worry, but I spent the whole time praying—not that he would succeed, but that *Bisavó* wouldn't make any more ill-tempered complaints.

I didn't doubt his success for a second, though I didn't know why. After all, he looked as if he were about my age, which Gordy confirmed. Something about him made me feel better. Come to think of it, there was really something about them all.

I learned they had been working closely together for months, and it showed. No one said this, but they were also clearly very close, like a family, though apparently only Shar and Khalid were actually related, and then only as foster siblings.

It wasn't that I was all alone in the world. I had my share of friends, and Gavin was a very good friend, one who probably would have risked himself for me too, if he had known I was in trouble.

The problem was that Gavin was friends with the person he thought I was. I realized as I watched these guys, who knew each other's secrets and accepted them, that Gavin didn't know me that way, would never know me that way, and that made me almost as sad as the poison inside of me. I guess that separation from everybody else was just a different kind of poison, a more subtle one.

At last Taliesin coaxed the light into an almost liquid form, and then dribbled some of it into the scratch on my arm. The scratch healed instantly, and I felt the droplets in my bloodstream. I was all warm inside, but a shudder ran through me as the light droplets hit the poison.

It wanted to struggle, to dig so deeply into my tissues that the light couldn't reach it; I knew that much instinctively. However, Shar's sword prevented it from doing anything to me, so it had nowhere to run. It screamed like the shadows as it shriveled up in the light.

"I'm cured!" I said happily before Taliesin could say anything, but he immediately agreed.

"So you are!" He and Viviane both smiled broadly, satisfied with a job well done.

Bisavó, who had been staring wistfully out to sea, was on me in a moment. "*Filho*!" she said joyfully, giving me an almost suffocating hug. The shift from great-grandson to son was not lost on me.

"What's next?" asked Shar, as if such miraculous cures were everyday events. Actually, for this group, they could be, for all I knew.

"More research, I think," replied Taliesin. "We beat that poison this time, but we needed two healers *and* a sword blessed by Apollo *and* a completely sunny environment with no shadows anywhere close...oh, and Shar's sword to hold the poison at bay. Plus, let's not forget that a normal human without Lucas's mixed lineage would have died long before we got there in the first place. We were lucky this time. We need a better way of dealing with this kind of thing."

"Taliesin, I can't thank you enough," I said.

"No problem, buddy...and it's Tal."

Since everyone had been calling him that for hours, I felt stupid for not picking up on it. Of course, I did have a few other things on my mind.

Suddenly I realized how tired I was. It must have been well after midnight back home.

"No rush," I said, "but I'd like to get back home when it's convenient."

Dead silence surrounded me. Even *Bisavó*, whom I might have expected to want the same thing, said nothing.

"Buddy, you can't go home...at least not right away," Tal said finally.

I looked at him but didn't respond, as if my brain were suddenly working at quarter speed.

"It wouldn't be safe," Tal continued when it became apparent that I wasn't going to say anything. "Until we can figure out how to keep the shadows out of this world, they'll keep coming at you. You'd be at risk every night. Even an overcast day might be a problem."

"Don't worry, Lucas. It was always my thought for you to come stay with me in the Encante," said *Bisavó*, putting her arm around me.

"What?" I said, still pretty slow on the uptake. "Before you even knew what the threat was?"

"I knew it was bad," she said quickly. "Bad enough that the human world might not be safe for you anymore. In the Encante, I can protect you. My people can protect you."

I struggled against fatigue and information overload. "What would my parents say to this?"

After another long silence, she said, "*Bisneto*, your mother could come with you if she wished. Your father, as I've told you before, has no supernatural blood. He would not be permitted."

"You…you want me to just leave Dad here?" I said, not really believing my own ears, even though I now remembered that earlier conversation about my dad.

"It may not have to be forever," said *Bisavó*, trying to be reassuring but missing the target by about a whole county.

"I am not leaving my *pai*!" I said emphatically.

"I know this is hard, *filho*, but what choice do we have?" she asked gently.

"I am not leaving my *pai*!" I repeated stubbornly and much more loudly.

At that moment, we heard a high, piercing shriek. I jumped and looked automatically in that direction.

The assassin—though it was hard to think of that frail-looking girl that way—had awakened. She was covering her face with her hands, probably because the sunlight was too bright for her, and she was shaking, perhaps from fear, perhaps from something else.

Bisavó stiffened. Gordy and Tal drew their swords, Khalid grabbed his bow, and Shar raised his fists. I stood there like an idiot, though I still clutched Shar's borrowed sword and could easily have raised it. Then, realizing I no longer needed the sword and wouldn't have been able to fight well with it anyway, I handed it back to Shar, who took it quickly and raised it, his eyes reflecting its green glow.

"She's not a threat," said Viviane quietly. "She can't see in this much light. I'll just put her back to sleep, and we can finish up here."

"Perhaps now is the time to discuss what we do with her," said Tal. That was definitely not what I wanted to talk about, but I was angry with *Bisavó*, not with him, and I held my peace. Maybe a little pause would give me time to figure out how to convince her that my place was in my own home.

"She could have valuable information," suggested Shar. "If we plan on fighting the shadows again, and we might have to, at the very least we should extract that information."

"Torture?" asked *Bisavó* in a surprisingly indifferent tone.

Tal looked offended. "We don't torture people. Anyway, we don't need to. I can read minds."

"I've never heard of anyone who could really do that," said *Bisavó*. Having seen what else Tal could do, I couldn't believe she questioned such a seemingly less spectacular ability.

"You aren't going to kill me?" the girl asked, her hands still over her face.

Bisavó said, "That remains to be seen," and, simultaneously, Tal said, "That depends on whether or not you intend to complete your mission."

"I have failed three times already," the girl said sadly. "Completing my trial now would be without meaning, for my existence will surely be ended when I return to the Populus Umbrae."

There was another long pause. Then Tal said, "As far as I can tell, she means what she says."

"Would you risk Lucas's life on a theory?" asked *Bisavó*, starting to sound belligerent again.

Tal looked at *Bisavó*, seemed to swallow his first idea for a response, and settled for, "She's our prisoner, not our friend. She's not going to be in a position to threaten us. That doesn't mean I intend to let the Populus Umbrae take her either."

"Nurse Florence," he said, turning to Viviane, "can you tell how the Populus Umbrae have altered her from the human norm?"

"I'm...I'm human?" the girl asked timidly.

"Perhaps," said Nurse Florence. She put her hand on the girl's shoulder. The defeated assassin flinched away from her touch, and then seemed to become resigned to it, though she was clearly frightened.

After a short time, Viviane said, "She's still basically human. Her eyes have been altered to allow her to see in the dark. The pallor is just a result of never being in the sun, not some physical change."

"That's it?" asked Tal, who was clearly expecting more.

"All physically," said Viviane. "But not spiritually. Her spirit is joined to the Shadow in the same way ours is joined to the Lake. That means she can use shadow magic and is much more agile in the dark than most humans. It also means the Populus Umbrae can definitely track her. They will reclaim her the moment she's in shadow."

"Can we break that bond?" asked Tal.

"Not without study," replied Viviane, looking puzzled.

"Mask it?"

"Possibly," she said, looking closely at the girl. "The chains in the cells at Awen, you know, the ones that prevent a captive from using magic, are designed to block even that kind of deep tie. After all, the designer had Ladies of the Lake very much in mind."

"You guys have cells?" I asked. Hey, it was a natural question at the time.

"Dude, we've got a whole dungeon!" said Gordy, as if he were describing a home entertainment system. "Some time we'll have to give you the tour."

"It's not really a dungeon, and an…associate of ours actually has it," corrected Tal. I didn't know if he was trying to be mysterious, but he made me even more curious.

"So, we chain her, and we…keep her in the light at all times, just to be sure, and then the Populus Umbrae won't be able to reclaim her," said Tal, thinking out loud.

"I don't think they can connect with her under those circumstances, but I can't guarantee it," said Nurse Florence. "Even the Order has very limited data on what these shadows can and cannot do."

My fatigue was catching up with me, to the point that I could hardly keep my eyes open, despite my odd circumstances. They actually fell shut for a second, but I forced them open. My vision…well, flickered is the best word, I guessed. Yeah, my vision flickered for a second, and then I noticed all of Tal's party had turned to me. Had I missed something?

"Lucas, it's time to head back home now," said *Bisavó*. "Say good-bye to your new friends."

"Home?" I said groggily. "But you said—"

"I was wrong," she admitted. "Of course you can't leave your father. We will find another way to keep you safe. Say good-bye now."

All of this seemed very sudden, but I decided to just go with it, even though I felt oddly reluctant to part with Tal and his friends. Maybe I would get to see them again some time. There was a *roda* coming up in Santa Barbara in about a month. I would have invited them, but my brain was still sluggish. Next thing I knew, they were waving good-bye, I was waving back, and then *Bisavó* and I turned toward a portal I didn't remember anyone opening. I could see Madisonville on the other side though. *Bisavó* put an arm around me and propelled me forward. Everything seemed like a dream. I must have been even more tired than I thought.

Suddenly I was nearly knocked off my feet by something that felt like an earthquake, and my vision rippled, a little like the earlier flicker, but much more violent, as if someone were tearing everything I was seeing apart.

Abruptly gone was the portal leading to Madisonville. Instead, I found myself standing waist-deep in the ocean, moving toward what appeared to be an archway made from the seawater itself. Beyond that arch was not Madisonville, but a luminous undersea scene, from which dolphin-like creatures stared back at me.

The Encante!

Bisavó had cast some kind of spell on me to get me to see what she wanted—and she had lied to me! She had no intention of letting me go back home.

"You will not take him against his will!" I heard Tal shouting. "And you will not use your illusions on any of us again!"

I looked back to the beach from which I had come. There was a sort of battle going on, with Tal and Viviane on one side, and *Bisavó* on the other. They weren't close physically, but even from where I was, I could feel power flowing back and forth between them. No, not flowing. More like surging, seething. Two forces wrestled with each other on that beach.

I started to move back toward the beach, but I was grabbed roughly by both arms. Two really muscular guys had come up from behind me. That could only mean one thing; they had come through the doorway from the Encante. They must be friends of *Bisavó*, here to make sure I couldn't get away if her illusion failed.

I had always thought I could take care of myself if I faced an attacker, but here was a situation for which I had no real training. Capoeira relied heavily on leg movements I had never tried to execute standing on sand, let alone in water, and the arm movements certainly didn't assume somebody had already restrained my arms. My extra speed wouldn't help either, unless I could get away from these guys, who were both stronger than I and pulling me in the direction of the doorway.

I had to do something fast. Once through that door, I had no idea if I could ever escape.

I looked back at the beach. Tal and Viviane both had strong magic, but *Bisavó* was apparently no slouch either. It looked as if she were losing whatever mystic struggle was going on, but it could be another couple of minutes before she lost completely, and by that time, I might be in the Encante. Shar, Gordy, and Khalid all stood there with stupid smiles plastered on their faces, apparently still in the grip of *Bisavó's* illusion. From what I'd been told, Shar's sword should have protected him, so she must have looked carefully to make sure he wasn't touching it before she struck. Bottom line: I wasn't getting any help for at least a while. I needed to slow these guys down if I wanted to stay in this world.

With my arms held securely in my kidnapper's vicelike hands, all I could do was kick, but even making a decent kick seemed unlikely. Most capoeira kicks derived their force from momentum and weren't normally executed while standing still. Also, I couldn't get my footing as the Encantados dragged me over wet sand, making it hard to get much force into a standing kick, and any kick I made would be slowed by the water even if it had force behind it.

Desperate, I pretended to pass out and went completely limp. Assuming these two were friends of *Bisavó* and didn't want me to come to harm, I figured they'd have to stop and check me.

Yeah, anyone who'd seen old movies would never have fallen for this move in a million years...but apparently the Encante didn't have ready access to the Hollywood classics. One of them took one of my arms in each hand, and I realized just how big those hands were. The other bent close to look me in the face and was, I think, about to do the old peel-back-the-eyelid-to-stare-into-the-eye routine.

Before he could, I went from limp back to struggling and gave him the strongest head butt I could manage. There wasn't much distance between us, hence not much force, but with my arms held and my feet slipping around, it was the best I could have hoped for.

The Encantado fell back a little, more from surprise than anything else, but that put him out of action for a couple seconds. I needed to make those seconds count. I couldn't beat both of them under these circumstances.

The other Encantado continued to grip my arms, but with less force, and there was a big difference between two guys each gripping one arm and one trying to manage both. Catching my captor by surprise, I tore my right arm free before he could tighten his grip. Then, finally able to exploit my speed, I hit him with a *cotovelada*, an elbow strike that would be better than a punch when we were still so close together. As surprised as his friend, he let go of my other arm, and I hit him with a *telefone*, simultaneous slaps to both ears that caused a sudden increase in air pressure inside his ear canals and disoriented him momentarily.

My opponents were far more used to the water than I was. Moving the fight to the beach was my best bet, but, with my first target recovered and reaching for me, I had to act fast. On land I could have outrun him easily, but I wasn't sure how fast I could run with my legs under water, so I dove in and swam as fast as I could until the water became too shallow. At that point I stood up and ran the rest of the way clumsily, but fast enough to do the job.

By now, the situation on shore had changed in Tal's favor. *Bisavó* had stopped fighting anyway. Looking more closely, I sensed Tal and Viviane's magic around her, preventing her from trapping them in illusions again. Shar, Gordy, and Khalid were also free. Khalid was now so alert that he aimed an arrow at the Encantados.

Turning, I noticed my would-be kidnappers were actually not pursuing with much enthusiasm.

Bisavó noticed their half-hearted chase as well. "What are you doing?" she asked in Portuguese.

"Thinking twice about tangling with *o diabo* there," one of them answered. "You didn't mention how much of a warrior he was."

"I didn't know it until today," *Bisavó* replied without any hint of apology in her tone.

"Wait!" I interrupted, already angry with her and realizing there might be yet another reason for that feeling. "You planned this before today...before we had even met."

"I knew you were in great danger." She was still unapologetic. "I always knew the need to take you to the Encante might arise."

"And you just pretended to think of the idea when we were talking. You always knew you would take me there no matter what," I said bitterly. "You always knew you would take me there by force. *Bisavó*, you call me a man, but you treat me like a child."

Instead of responding to me, she turned her attention back to Tal. "You will allow me to take Lucas with me, or my people will come through the door I have opened and overwhelm you with their power!"

"I'm sure you have friends and family who might answer your call, but your whole people?" asked Viviane skeptically. "There was never been a mass attack by the Encantado in all of recorded history."

"Nor of *pessoas da sombra*," *Bisavó* replied. "Times change."

Turning to her friends, still wavering in the surf, she commanded, "Wrap them in illusion!"

"Shar!" called Tal. "Why don't you wade out a little way and help our new friends find their way back to the Encante?"

With an emerald flash, Shar drew his sword and headed for the waves. I felt *Bisavó's* allies try to trap him in illusion, but the sword protected him. When they realized he wasn't vulnerable to their magic, they seamlessly shifted into dolphin form and swam like hell for the doorway. Shar followed, waited until they had fled, and then slashed his sword through the doorway, causing it to collapse in an emerald flash.

"Lovers, not fighters," observed Gordy and snickered.

Thinking about what *Bisavó* had told me of the habits of her people, I realized he was probably right.

"Tal," Khalid said nervously, "the girl's gone!"

Every eye focused on where she had been. Khalid was right.

Tal closed his eyes for a second. "Shar, Gordy, Khalid, she's headed for the castle. She can't get in, but the castle obviously throws a shadow, and if she stands in it, maybe she can reconnect with her people."

"We're on it," said Gordy, and then he and Shar trotted off in the direction of the castle, with Khalid flying above them, arrows ready.

"This is your fault," Tal pointed out to *Bisavó*. "She escaped while you were keeping us busy."

"She wouldn't have escaped if she'd been dead," *Bisavó* retorted.

"It really doesn't matter, does it?" Viviane asked tiredly. "They'll bring her back, and then we can…"

She stopped, and I figured she was about to say, "go home," and then realized that I still couldn't.

"What's going to happen to me?" I tried not to sound too pathetic. "I'm not leaving my family," I added firmly, "and I'm not going somewhere I can't have a real life."

Tal pondered for a minute. "I doubt the shadows can track you now that the poison is out of your system, but they still know where you live. I suppose, in theory, your family could move somewhere else, but if you go back to your house to pack, they will be watching, and they can follow you after that, even in daylight, as long as they have some dark corner to watch from. Your whole family would have to be extremely cautious on the trip—difficult to arrange, since you can't tell your dad what's really happening."

"I can't tell my dad?" I repeated stupidly.

"I've mentioned this before. Why do you think I had to put him to sleep?" asked *Bisavó*. "All supernatural societies have one thing in common: we can't let ordinary humans know about us. Occasionally, exceptions can be made, but they often take time to set up…time we don't have. Months, maybe."

"My own dad doesn't know about my…unusual abilities," Tal said. I must still have looked pretty confused, because he added, "My mom knows only because she became a seer and figured it out on her own."

"Your own dad doesn't know about you?" I said, still having a hard time believing what I was hearing.

"Does yours know about you?" asked Tal. "You didn't even know you weren't supposed to tell, but you didn't, right?"

"I didn't…because…because I…"

"Felt like a freak?" offered Tal. "Dude, I know. But part of your not telling may also be hard-coded into your mind somehow. I can't find many records of someone with unusual abilities connected to the supernatural world, particularly related to supernatural ancestry, who willingly told anyone. That can't be coincidence."

I wanted to ask him where his abilities came from, but the trio returned with the recaptured assassin.

"She made it to the shadow," said Khalid before anyone else could speak. "I…I couldn't bring myself to shoot her."

Bisavó grumbled but fortunately did not say anything.

"Well, she's still here," said Tal, "so perhaps her people didn't have time to make a connection."

"I'm still alive," said the assassin, so clearly she didn't think her people had connected either.

I was surprised at the indifference of her tone, so flat that, if it really reflected her feelings, she was already resigned to death. I shouldn't have cared, but I felt sad about her.

"Well, now we've solved every problem except the biggest one," said Viviane. "How do we keep Lucas safe but still let him have a normal life?"

"Let's take him with us," Gordy suggested.

Shar laughed in a fairly uncomplimentary way, but Tal actually seemed to consider the idea. "We could relocate his whole family that way."

"What good would that do?" asked *Bisavó.*

I had to admit she had a point this time. Why would moving to Santa Brígida be any different from moving anywhere else?

Tal spent a couple seconds trying to frame an answer that wouldn't start another argument, but Gordy jumped right in. "Lady, you have no idea who you're dealing with, do you? Not even after what you've seen today? Tal isn't some clueless teenager fumbling his way from one mess to another. He has the knowledge and skills from all of his previous lives at his fingertips. He was the original Taliesin in King Arthur's court. If he thinks we can keep Lucas safe, we can."

"That's enough, Gordy," said Tal, a little embarrassed.

"He was also Alexander the Great's right-hand man. He fought with Achilles at Troy. He was friends with King David of Israel," said Gordy, pressing on.

"Gordy!" said Tal, but it was clear that Gordy was sick of *Bisavó* and determined to get her to admit she was wrong.

"And that's not all!" he continued even more loudly. "Three other members of our group can also draw on their pasts. Not me," he added, almost apologetically, "but Shar has been Alexander…and Achilles. Stan and Carla, who aren't here right now, were once King David and the sorceress Alcina, who created this island centuries ago."

Twenty-four hours ago I would have thought Gordy was nuts. Now his rant sounded almost normal.

"I have heard of Alcina," said *Bisavó* grudgingly, as if she hadn't heard of all the others. "But I'm not as interested in the past as I am in the present."

"And in the present, there are issues to consider," said Viviane, probably trying to redirect the conversation. "Tal, are you thinking about locking Santa Brígida down completely? You know how much energy covering an area that large takes. We can't do it for more than a few days."

"I haven't forgotten," Tal replied. "What I'm thinking is maximum protection for a couple days while we work out a more specific plan to keep out the Populus Umbrae. A more narrowly defined defense could cover a large area without using nearly as much power, right?"

"We've already got all of our houses pretty well covered," pointed out Shar. "We could do the same for the house his family moves into, right? And there's at least some protection on the school already."

"If we can find a defense against the Populus Umbrae and cover the whole town with it, we just might be able to pull this off," Viviane conceded.

"Wait!" I said quickly. "I don't want to sound ungrateful, but what about all my friends?"

"It's not like you'll never see them again," said Tal. "You aren't going to be so far away that visits are out of the question, though it will be much better if you get them to visit you in Santa Brígida."

"Once we have a magic that keeps the shadows away, we can probably get…one of our supernatural blacksmith friends…to make you a bracelet or something that gives the same kind of protection to you personally," said Tal, "and then you can go visit them too, or go pretty much wherever you want."

"Supernatural blacksmiths?" OK, there were more important things to talk about, but I had to ask.

"We're tight with Hephaestus," said Gordy, waving his sword a little, as if I had missed his point. "Oh, and Govannon, the smith for the Welsh faeries too. Between the two of them, we've got gear you wouldn't believe."

From what I'd seen, he was not exaggerating.

"Why would a group of humans be so favored?" *Bisavó* asked suspiciously. I had so hoped that she would just keep her mouth shut until this was over. Apparently, she was going to keep right on embarrassing me. I'd never seen a worse case of looking a gift horse in the mouth…or maybe I should have said gift dragon.

"Because we're badasses," offered Gordy—hardly an explanation *Bisavó* would likely accept, and possibly not even understand.

"He means we impressed Gwynn ap Nudd, the king of the Welsh faeries, when he tested us," said Shar in a matter-of-fact way. "The Olympians helped us, but we helped them quite a bit as well. Actually, we prevented a major disruption of the Olympian plane."

I prayed that *Bisavó* would not question them any further. She still looked dissatisfied, but, to my enormous relief, she kept her continued doubts to herself—at least for now.

I couldn't visualize Gavin being five hours away; we'd grown up together. Tal and his friends were trying awfully hard to help me, so I didn't have the nerve to gripe about leaving my best friend behind. Still, there was one problem I didn't see any way around.

"It sounds like a well thought-out plan," I said, "but there's no way my dad will move at the drop of a hat. Anyway, his work is in Merced. He's been with the same architectural firm for twenty years...and they're based there. He can't very well commute from the Santa Barbara area, and he's unlikely to find a job good enough to make him want to switch to another firm."

"An architect?" asked Tal. "Tell me about his work."

I couldn't imagine how the details of what my dad did could possibly help, but I told Tal everything I could remember. He seemed especially pleased to learn that my dad had designed a couple of buildings in Santa Barbara.

"I think I can solve your dad problem, but I need to leave for a few minutes," Tal said.

"What about our...guest?" asked Viviane, tilting her head toward *Bisavó.*

"She will swear an oath not to take any hostile action, nor to try to take Lucas against his will," said Tal as if she had already agreed.

"There are ways to bind supernatural beings with oaths," said Gordy for my benefit.

Don't be difficult; please, don't be difficult!

"What if I refuse such an oath?" she asked. I wondered what would happen if Tal finally got sick of dealing with her.

Tal was evidently keeping his temper on a short leash, because his voice sounded controlled. "Santa Brígida is near the coast. You can visit Lucas there much more easily than you can in Madisonville. On the other hand, it would be relatively easy for us to ward the area against full-blooded Encantados, and you'd never see him at all."

Bisavó had done just fine not seeing me for the first sixteen years of my life, so I expected her to scoff at that threat. Much to my surprise, she looked shocked, and I swore I saw a tear as she and Tal worked out the specifics of the oath. She wanted him to swear that as long as she cooperated with him, he would never prevent her from seeing me. In the end, they did some kind of binding spell that Gordy told me was called a *tynged* in Welsh, and I felt it settle around them when they were done.

And adults say that teenagers are unpredictable!

It seemed like only a few minutes after Tal vanished into a portal that he reappeared the same way, with a big smile on his face.

"Tomorrow, right at the opening of business, your dad's firm is going to get a call from Carrie Winn."

"As in Winn Industries?" I asked.

"The same," he replied. "She's going to offer the firm an insanely lucrative contract to develop plans for several buildings in the Santa Barbara area. She's going to insist, though, that she needs close communication with the architect on the project, and she will name your dad as the only one she'll accept, based on his outstanding designs that she's seen in Santa Barbara. That collaboration will be so close that your dad will have to move to the area, specifically, into a house in Santa Brígida that he and his family will live in rent-free. Winn will apologize for the short notice but will insist he gets down to Santa Brígida to meet with her by the next day."

"How can we get packed that fast?"

"She'll suggest that you each take only what you absolutely need. She'll send an assistant up to Madisonville to supervise the packing and moving of all the rest."

I was stunned. "Tal, that sounds great, but...but...it's too incredible to believe. Even if my dad's partners somehow buy it, I don't think he will."

"I've found people often believe what they want to believe," Tal replied. "One of the wealthiest people in California turns out to be a great fan of your dad's work—will he really stop to question that? Besides...look, I didn't mean to pry, but I did catch some of your thoughts while I was healing you. Madisonville's really not that great a place, is it?"

I nodded.

"Well, is he that big a fan of it?"

"He really enjoys his job," I said, "but living in Madisonville is something he does because he has to."

"So he gets handed a reason to move on a silver platter, and he gets to keep the same job…and his firm gets rich. Again, is he really going to question that?"

"I guess not," I said, still trying to absorb it all. "How did you do all that so fast?"

"Shall we tell him?" asked Shar. "If he's going to be one of us, he'll need to know anyway."

Tal and Viviane both nodded.

"One of you?" I asked. That part intrigued me even more than whatever revelation they had about Carrie Winn.

"As much as you want to be," said Tal. "You're leaving some friends behind, I know…but if you want to hang with us, you can."

"There won't be any awkward new-guy adjustment period if you're with us," Gordy said. "I don't want to sound too cocky, but among us, we pretty much know everyone, and we're well liked. If you're with us, everybody will treat you as if you've always been there. Some will do it for superficial reasons, but a lot will do it for real."

"And, consider this," added Gordy. "There's no lack of hot girls, and every so often, one realizes she doesn't have a shot with Tal and becomes available."

Tal blushed noticeably at that.

"How could I not be sold?" I laughed.

"On the more serious side, you can train with us if you want, become more versatile," said Shar, whom I recalled had a mixed martial-arts background. "If you want, you could also teach us some of those capoeira moves."

"Isn't capoeira basically like dance?" asked Gordy. I didn't know him well enough to be sure whether he was kidding or actually putting me down. He'd been very friendly, but I was pretty tired of people ridiculing my choice of a martial art.

Then I did something profoundly stupid. With a sweeping kick, I knocked him off his feet and sent him tumbling to the sand. It wasn't an astute move. I could have made an enemy of someone I'd need as a friend.

Shar laughed heartily, and I breathed a sigh of relief when Gordy joined him. "Good one, man!" he said happily, still sitting on the sand. "Really good one!"

I don't know what, but something about these guys made me feel as if I'd known them for years, rather than hours. I would really miss Gavin...but I could get used to this group very, very quickly.

Well, that is, if *Bisavó* didn't find some way to blow the whole deal.

"I see how it is," she said, even more suspiciously than before. "You want to use Lucas for his skills. This isn't about protecting him; it's about giving yourselves another man in combat!"

Tal did a masterful job of covering up the fact that she had really offended him, but the look in his eyes gave him away. "This is about protecting Lucas. If he were a ninety-eight pound weakling, he'd have gotten the same treatment. If he wants to join us when there's a threat, he's welcome, but our help doesn't have strings attached."

I swallowed my annoyance with her as best I could. "*Bisavó*, coming here to warn me was risky for you, wasn't it?"

"I didn't know what threatened you, *Bisneto*, so in that sense, yes it was," she replied.

"Yet you came, even though you didn't really know me."

"I did know you!" she shot back, sounding almost angry. "My people thought it best I not visit, but I have watched you since the moment you were born. I was there the first time you tried capoeira. I was there for your first kiss—"

"Wow, not creepy at all!" said Gordy.

Bisavó looked intensely irritated by the interruption, and I knew I had to intervene to prevent another argument...no doubt, an embarrassing one.

"So you came because I'm family, because you love me," I said.

"Yes, of course!" she replied.

"Well, all these people came, more or less on the spur of the moment, to help a total stranger. They saved me...and all you've done is give them attitude the whole time. You have to stop it!"

"But—" she began.

"No, stop it!" I said, as if I were ordering a child...not the way I was taught to respect elders, but I had just met her tonight, and she had spent most of that time not acting grandmotherly. Oh, and there was that kidnap attempt. I wasn't going to beat myself up for being too harsh.

"You know what?" I continued. "They helped me…and I'm going to help them…whether you like it or not!" Turning to Tal and the guys, I added, "I would be honored to be one of you."

I had deterred *Bisavó* from ripping into Gordy, but she wasn't quite done yet.

"Meaning no disrespect," she said in a tone that missed sincerity by a mile or so, "your plan leaves Lucas exposed for another day."

"I didn't think we could sell a midnight phone call from Carrie Winn or a demand for Lucas's father to drive all night to get to Santa Brígida," said Tal evenly. "I'll stay in Madisonville with him—invisibly, so as not to freak out his dad or anyone else. I'll escort them on the drive down also."

"You can run as fast as the car?" I asked. With this guy, it was hard to know whether he had any limits. Certainly, none were obvious.

"I can use magic to accelerate to faerie speed—roughly comparable to what you can do, I think, except it's natural for you. But no, I can't keep up with a car on the highway. I can also use magic to fly, and that's how I think I'll follow. It's going to be kind of a strain to fly that far; I'm really only used to short distances. I'm sure I can do it though."

Yet another explanation I would have thought insane only twenty-four hours ago. Now it seemed completely rational, almost run-of-the-mill.

I half expected *Bisavó* to take issue with the last part, but she said nothing. Maybe she finally realized that I was in good hands. More likely, she had figured out she wasn't getting anywhere and just bowed to the inevitable. At this point, I'd take that!

It wasn't too long before Viviane, Shar, Gordy, and Khalid said their good-byes and left. Viviane promised to make sure the house was ready for my family, and the guys said they'd organize some kind of party to welcome me to town so that I could meet people and get comfortable as soon as possible.

By this point it was something like two o'clock in the morning back in Madisonville, and, again, I could hardly keep my eyes open. I wanted to go home, but Tal thought it was too dangerous and suggested we get a little sleep on the beach, protected by broad daylight and distant from any shadows cast by the castle. I would much rather have slept in bed at home, but then I realized I couldn't sleep worrying about someone leaping out of the shadows and attacking me. I'd have to sleep with all the lights on and the closet open to avoid any possibility of attack, and, as Tal was quick to point out, if the girl we captured today wasn't the only human the shadows had kidnapped and trained, light alone might not protect me. Somewhat grumpily I lay down on the sand, but I basically passed out within minutes.

Chapter 9: Like a Dream (Lucas)

Tal woke me a few hours later. We needed to get me back home so that I could go to school and my dad wouldn't realize something weird had happened.

Bisavó could have left with the others but insisted on staying. I'm not sure whether she watched over me while I slept, explored the island, or waded out to sea and became a dolphin for a while. The important thing was that she now seemed reconciled to my going to Santa Brígida, even happy about it. I knew she had taken some kind of oath not to interfere, but that agreement didn't require her to pretend to like the arrangement. I wasn't sure what had happened to change her mind, but, frankly, I didn't care, as long as she didn't embarrass me again…or try to kidnap me!

It didn't take Tal long to get us back to Madisonville by portal. *Bisavó* bustled off to lift the sleep spells on Mon and Dad while I grabbed a quick shower…with Tal standing guard right outside the bathroom door. I supposed that could have been creepy, but I already felt like I knew him, and I didn't have to worry about shadows with him that close.

There would have been no easy way to explain Tal's presence to my dad, so he made himself invisible and watched (probably hungrily) while the rest of us ate breakfast. Mom looked relieved, so I figured *Bisavó* had briefed her on the plan, and Mom must have been OK with it. Of course, that also meant *Bisavó* must have made it sound like a good thing, and that was more evidence that she had accepted it herself. Everything was coming together nicely.

The school day passed like a blur. I said good-bye to my friends, and that was hard, especially with Gavin. The dancers weren't that happy either, particularly since we had a show coming up, but, all things considered, the day went about as well as could be expected.

Almost at the end of the day, though, I realized I might have blown it big-time.

"Tal," I whispered. He was nearby, invisible, as he had been all day.

"Yeah, buddy?" he whispered back.

"I said good-bye to people and told them about my dad's new job, but it'll be awkward if he somehow hears about that. He didn't know about the change himself when I left for school, and he hasn't called me yet. There's no way I could have known about it."

"I would have stopped you if I thought it was a problem," he said reassuringly.

"But I told Janice, and her mom works with him. She could very easily—"

"You worry too much," Tal said, sounding almost like Gordy. "Your dad would have found out as soon as he got to work, and neither Janice nor her mom will know he didn't call you right away. They have no reason to worry about it or ask him about it. Chill!"

What Tal was saying made sense, but the way he said it made me uneasy. Last night he hadn't exactly come across as a total stress case, but he was clearly not as laid back as Gordy. I'd seen Tal's type before. I figured him for the kind of guy who didn't exactly obsess, but who was meticulous about details. He didn't seem quite that way now.

I was probably being silly. I hadn't even known him for a whole day, so how could I really judge if he was being himself or not?

I got Dad's call right after my last class, asking me to come home right away so we could talk. I pretended to be resistant to missing dance rehearsal, so he wouldn't get suspicious, but I agreed quickly when he told me he really needed to see me.

When I got home, he told me about the sudden change in his job, and, despite my earlier misgivings, he didn't seem to suspect that there was more to this new development than he had been told.

I wasn't surprised when *Bisavó* announced she wanted to come with us and see our new home; she probably still wanted to keep an eye on me. I was pleasantly surprised that Dad's head didn't explode. In fact, he and she seemed to be getting along like...well, like family. Last night's tension was completely forgotten.

Just as Carrie Winn had asked, we each packed a few things we'd need for tomorrow. By the time we finished, a Winn Industries employee popped by to assure my parents that he'd make sure everything else was properly packed and shipped to us. Then we loaded the car and hit the road. Since we had a five-hour drive ahead, Dad wanted to start as early as we could and have dinner on the way.

The trip, like the school day, seemed a little fuzzy. I was both tired and excited, so it didn't surprise me that I was a little out of it.

About midway through the trip, though, I began to worry about Tal. During one of our conversations, Shar or Gordy mentioned that magic burned energy at a pretty constant rate. Tal had exerted heavily last night, gotten little sleep, and stayed invisible the whole school day. He still had to be invisible now…and fly. He'd told me that since he was human and not faerie or djinn, flying required energy too. I didn't think he'd eaten anything today either. What would happen if he ran out of juice?

I must have been in a weird mood, because I started imagining Tal plunging out of the sky and smashing his skull open right in front of us. It wasn't one of my visions, but once I started thinking about it, it was hard to get out of my mind. The worst part was that I had no way to check with him to make sure he was still all right. I found myself watching the road in front of us, half-expecting that Icarus-style plunge I kept imagining.

Fortunately, we reached Santa Brígida without incident. Once there, we were greeted with everything but a marching band and a twenty-one gun salute. Carrie Winn was waiting for us at our new address, as was the mayor, several other dignitaries, and a big crowd of high school students. I hadn't thought Gordy and Shar meant to have a party tonight, but there it was, so I went with it. My parents threw themselves into the adult meet and greet.

It took me a few minutes to realize something was wrong.

I'd been to Santa Barbara, but never to Santa Brígida. The guys hadn't really described it to me, either, except in very general terms. Tal made some comment about Spanish colonial-revival architecture, for example. There sure was plenty of that, but the streets we had traveled to reach our new house seemed somehow familiar. It wasn't until after we'd arrived and I was in the midst of the party that I realized why.

They were all streets I'd seen in Santa Barbara.

What were the odds that part of the layout of Santa Brígida was the same as Santa Barbara's? Similar, maybe, but exactly the same, down to the street names? And I knew Santa Brígida was a lot smaller. The trip to the house took longer than it should have. We had spent twenty minutes driving from the town border to our house, which wasn't clear on the other side of town.

Then there was the house itself. It had looked oversized for the neighborhood, but I figured Carrie Winn had pulled out all the stops and gotten us the biggest place available. My dad had taught me enough about architecture to question the way the house fit into the neighborhood though. I knew that Santa Brígida, like many new developments, had a lot of houses, but just a few basic floor plans, and all the houses would be pretty close to the same size, at least in the same neighborhood. No sane developer would drop a mansion into the middle of a block with more modest homes. Sometimes neighborhoods evolved that way through remodeling, but they would never be planned that way.

Then there were the guests. Aside from the people I had already met, they looked...well, too good to be true is the best way I can put it. The girls, especially, looked like Central Casting's answer to the female population of a high school. I remembered Gordy telling me there were hot girls, and certainly Viviane, though somewhat older, was as hot as any guy could want, but no population was composed exclusively of good-looking people...except sometimes on TV or in the movies.

Looking more closely, I realized that, except for the people I'd met last night and my own family, almost everyone reminded me of some actor or actress I'd seen. One or two people would have been understandable, but everyone?

There was only one possible explanation: I was dreaming. The only problem with that explanation was that everything around me was so realistic, so detailed. It had been totally believable when I had been at home. Only now, when I was in unfamiliar territory, and I assumed my subconscious was fleshing out the detail from random memories, could I see clearly that what I was seeing couldn't be real. My mind—or maybe someone else, come to think of it—was feeding me some fantasy version of Santa Brígida: I lived in a mansion; every single kid at my school had flocked to greet me; and the girls, if I was only going by appearances, looked like every teenage guy's fantasies. Oh, and my dad and *Bisavó* were getting along as if they had known and liked each other for years.

After all the stress of yesterday, there was a part of me that just wanted to go with it—and there was a lot of "it" to go with. A number of girls were eying me. How easy it would be to take one of them upstairs to my new bedroom, which, judging by the rest of the house, probably had satin sheets, and have wild sex with her. Actually, given the size of the house, the bed was probably big enough for more than two of us. The possibilities were endless.

Well, at least they would have been if I were all hormones and no brain. The balance was a little off for a minutes, but there was still some brain in the mix. I supposed a dream this vivid could be caused by magic, and that suggested someone had me under a spell—*Bisavó,* most likely—though how she got around her oath I couldn't guess. If I were right, I couldn't see any purpose for it...unless I was being kidnapped again, and I couldn't let that happen. The Encante might be beautiful. It might even be safe. But every instinct told me it would never be home.

Impulsively, I sought out Tal, who appeared to be sucking face with some Selena Gomez clone. That was another thing that didn't make sense. If this really had been our house in Santa Brígida, it would probably have some magic protection, but Tal didn't seem like the kind of guy who would just take for granted that I was safe and slip away to stick his tongue down some girl's throat.

I coughed and said, "Tal, can I talk to you for a minute?"

"Sure," he replied. "Excuse us for a minute, will you, honey?"

The girl nodded, smiled, and walked away.

That scene was yet another flaw in the scenario. If Tal *had* been the kind of guy to slip away for some quick fun, he would have been annoyed by the interruption. I knew I would have been under similar circumstances. His...girlfriend, I guessed, probably would have been too. Instead, they both acted like my needs should always come first...just the way I would want it in some fantasy.

"So what's up?" he asked. "You look worried."

"It's not really a big deal. I just remembered you guys were going to tell me something about Carrie Winn, something important, and never got the chance to. What was it?"

Tal looked blank for a second. "I don't really remember having anything important to say about her, but that was a pretty hectic night. I'm sure it'll come back to me after I get rested up. Anything else?"

"No, thanks. That was all," I said.

"Well, then, back to business," he said with a wink, heading off to find the Selena Gomez clone, still without any worry about the shadows, or whether or not whatever protection was on the house would hold.

Now I knew for sure that what was happening around me wasn't real. There was something about Carrie Winn, something secret enough for Shar to ask permission to tell me, something important enough he'd figured I'd need to know. Yet now Tal had no idea what I was talking about. He couldn't, of course, because he wasn't Tal but just an image thrown together by my subconscious. If I didn't know something, he couldn't either. That's why my surroundings were so unrealistic. My mind was building them out of conjecture and creepy wish fulfillment.

The other guys in Tal's group, the ones I hadn't met yet, weren't here, but that made sense too, since I hadn't met them. Shar, Gordy, and Khalid were here, so I tried the Carrie Winn question on them and got almost exactly the same response I had from Tal.

Fake! Everything, everyone around me was fake!

OK, I knew the truth, but now what? I tried willing myself to wake up, but nothing happened. I guessed if there was a spell on me, it would take more than just wishing to be awake to wake up. But what?

I tried to remember every word I'd been told, but we hadn't really talked about sleep spells, even though I'd seen one in action.

What about Tal? There was a phony one in here with me, but he wouldn't be any help. What about the real Tal though? He had been with me on the beach.

I shuddered as a new dark thought popped up.

What if he were dead?

I tried to talk myself out of that idea. *Bisavó* had her faults, and she had been ready to kill the shadow assassin girl, but Tal had been trying to protect me, not kill me. Surely *Bisavó* couldn't be that much of a monster…could she?

I tried to think about *Mestre* Ribeiro's advice. He had always said focus was the most important thing in capoeira, but often in life too. I needed to put my churning emotions in check and figure out what to do if I wanted to avoid being trapped in the Encante for the rest of my life.

The most likely assumption was that Tal was still alive, just under a spell. I didn't know how to break out of a magic dream like this, but he might…if he realized he was dreaming. What if his mind was running the same kind of scenario mine was? There would have been glitches in the way he saw Madisonville, because he had only seen a little of it, and that at night. However, if he were focused on watching me, he might not have noticed discrepancies. If he hadn't noticed then, he certainly wouldn't notice later, back in Santa Brígida, when his mind could have given him much greater realism.

If I was still on that beach, if I hadn't already been taken to the Encante, he was probably still near me physically. There wouldn't really be any point in maintaining this dream once I was in the Encante and couldn't get away, so I had to hope I was still on the beach or, at worst, being floated out to one of those watery doorways.

OK, Tal was probably still nearby. So what, if he hadn't realized he was locked in a dream? How could I get word to him?

I was forgetting something! I knew I was, but I couldn't make it come back. I was stuck.

I tried to stay calm, and finally I remembered. Tal had mentioned being able to read minds, had apologized for picking up some of my thoughts while he was healing me. I knew being asleep and dreaming didn't preclude magic; I myself had experienced visions of the future while asleep on one or two occasions. Tal wasn't actively reading anyone's mind, or he would already know he was in a dream, but he might still have the ability to read them.

I knew the idea was crazy, but I kept thinking that if I could get myself to broadcast my thoughts to him, maybe I could get him to wake up. I had never tried anything like that, and maybe I couldn't broadcast strongly enough to reach him, but what else did I have? Nothing. If the idea didn't work, I was screwed.

I tried to focus all my energy into one simple thought, *Tal, you're dreaming!* If I could get him to hear that, he would realize what was happening. Worth a shot, anyway.

I don't know if what happened next was built into the spell or just coincidence, but people kept bugging me while I tried to concentrate, girls mostly, and I swore they were wearing less clothing each time. The adults seemed to have disappeared, and the house had turned into teenage party central. Yeah, definitely not real! I sighed.

Not knowing what else to do, I ran outside and switched to high speed to get away from all the noise and distraction, hormonal and otherwise. Luckily, no one followed me. In real life, of course, someone would have, if only to make sure the shadows weren't eating me.

I put a few blocks of half-remembered Santa Barbara streets between me and the house. Then I sat down on the sidewalk and threw every brain cell I had into projecting that one message.

I pushed until my head throbbed. I pushed until I felt like I would start bleeding out of my ears. I pushed until I had almost nothing left to push with.

Then, very, very faintly, I heard Tal's voice or probably his thoughts.

"Lucas?"

"It's me!" I yelled. *"I'm stuck in a dream. You must be too. Can you break us out?"*

I didn't get an immediate answer and was afraid he had sunk back into his dream or couldn't break free. Then the "reality" around me shuddered, became unfocused. It snapped back after a few seconds, but at least I knew Tal was working on it.

He gave the world I was trapped in several more jolts. Each time, it reasserted itself but a little fuzzier, a little less convincing. On the last hit, it dissolved, and I was blinking my eyes against the sun on the beach.

"You can't do this!" *Bisavó* said. At first, I thought she was talking to Tal.

"Keep your eyes shut!" Tal's thoughts boomed in my head. *"Let me figure out what we're dealing with before you do anything."*

"You do nothing but talk about this brat!" said a deep male voice. "I'm sick of it! He comes back with us...now. Then you can pay some attention to me again!"

"Vitor, I gave my word!" protested *Bisavó*. Unless this were some kind of act, I was being kidnapped again...but not by her this time.

"There are three of them," Tal thought to me, *"and each has a fair amount of power. To keep from getting caught in another dream or illusion, I need you to attack them physically so their attention will be divided. Are you in condition to fight?"*

"Absolutely!" I thought back.

"Now!" Tal thought. I opened my eyes and leaped up, ready to do battle with Vitor and his cronies. Tal was also up, and I felt him sending a major blast of power their way.

Though the Encantados looked tough, kind of like thugs from some dubious neighborhood in Rio, they weren't much of a match for Tal and me. I couldn't escape the feeling they had never seen capoeira, and I had no trouble knocking them down like dominoes. Their magic might have been another matter, but with Tal—and, to my pleasant surprise, *Bisavó*—hitting them hard with enough mystic force to beat twice their number, it was only a few minutes before they fled into the ocean, became dolphins, and swam frantically for the exit door.

Bisavó sighed loudly. "I'm sorry, Lucas. I thought Vitor was a different person from the one we saw today."

"People will do strange things for love," Tal said, oddly understanding. "Vitor was trying to get himself out of second place."

"I'm afraid it was more lust than love with Vitor." *Bisavó* eyed Tal as if she, too, were trying to figure out why he wasn't more angry with her.

"What you did, you did because you care about Lucas," Tal said, answering that very question. Perhaps she had been thinking about it too loudly. "I have to give you credit for that. I'm not even going to point out that Vitor's little stunt proves the Encante may not be as safe as you thought."

"I'm certainly glad you're not going to bring that up," *Bisavó* said, with just a hint of sarcasm…and a smile. Were these two actually starting to get along?

"Of course," she added, "I will expect to be consulted on all your plans for Lucas's safety."

"I wouldn't have it any other way." Tal's face was totally deadpan. I wondered if he wouldn't prefer that she just vanish into the Encante, never to return.

Tal glanced at his watch. "Fortunately, we didn't lose too much time on this little diversion. We should still be able to be back in Madisonville before dawn."

"Really?" I said, surprised. "I don't know about you, but I dreamed a whole day's worth of events."

"Yeah, but you took only a few minutes dreaming them," said Tal. "Dreams—and some of the other worlds—are funny that way."

As we prepared to leave, I said, "Tal, you guys were going to tell me something about Carrie Winn, and we never got back to that."

"We'll bring you up to speed on everything in the next few days," Tal said. "We probably shouldn't take the time now."

My stomach twisted. Could this be yet another layer of dream? "I know this will sound strange, but I really need you to tell me about her now."

Tal shrugged. "Well, if you'll settle for the short version, Carrie Winn isn't a real person. That's a fictitious identity created by Ceridwen as part of a plan to trap me. After we defeated her, one of our Lady-of-the-Lake allies, Vanora, took over the identity. Having someone rich and influential on our side has served us well many times, your dad's new job opportunities being a good example. Is that enough for now? We really should be going."

"That was great!" I said, having verified that I was actually talking to the real Tal and not some half-baked dream.

The first part of the real day went a little bit like my dream had, except that my mom slipped the invisible Tal food during breakfast, and my dad was still tense around *Bisavó*.

The school day seemed to drag, maybe partly because it felt like a rerun, though, naturally, all the details were different from the dream. The real Tal cautioned me against telling my friends I was leaving until my dad told me. I agreed with the wisdom of that advice, though it made the day relatively emotional at first. It was hard thinking that I might not be able to say good-bye to the people who were important to me. Fortunately, in contrast to the dream, Dad called about the middle of the day. All he wanted to do was ask me to come home right after school, but I pressed him, and he told me about the move to Santa Brígida, freeing me to say a proper good-bye.

Later that day, while I was packing for the move, I was alone with Tal for a few minutes, and I shared my concern about whether or not he could make the trip. Unlike the dream, he had been eating, but he had also had to use quite a bit of magic fighting off Vitor and company.

"Considering you didn't know anything about magic a day ago, you're a quick study." Tal gave me a pat on the back. "Yeah, being invisible and flying for a five-hour trip, let alone what's happened earlier, is a pretty big drain. That's why I'll have some help. Actually, let me introduce you." He then proceeded to expend even more energy, opening a portal and disappearing into it for a minute. When he returned, he had Khalid right behind him. The kid gave me a big hug, even though he hardly knew me. Right behind him was someone I hadn't met yet.

The new guy was dressed incongruously in the armor of an ancient Greek warrior, though I knew an ordinary human would probably see what he was wearing as street clothes. He was muscular but not especially good-looking.

"Khalid you know, of course. Lucas, this is Alex."

We shook hands.

"I was thinking the very same thing you were," Tal continued, "and I knew I needed backup. Khalid can become invisibly naturally, and his armor allows him to fly, as you've seen. Alex has...well, Alex, why don't you show him?"

Alex seemed to levitate right off the floor. Looking more closely I noticed his sandals had rapidly flapping wings.

"An extra pair Hermes had lying around," said Alex, as if what he was saying wasn't completely incredible.

I looked at Tal quizzically.

"It is, as Gordy would say, a long story," he replied to my unspoken question. "Don't worry, though; we'll fill you in on everything when we have the time. As you can see, Alex can fly on his own, though I will have to use some magic to keep him invisible. The three of us will be flying above you during the trip, and, if I get too tired, Celtic magic has several ways for people to share energy, so they can lend me some and keep me going. Besides, in the unlikely event that there is an attack, three of us would be a far better defense than one."

I wanted to press for the story behind the winged sandals, but Dad yelled to find out if I was ready to go yet. I yelled my yes back, grabbed the one bag I'd packed, and started to leave.

"We'll be above by the time you guys get loaded into the car," said Tal. "If you spot something that might be a problem, think about it as hard as you can, and I'll hear you."

I thanked him and headed downstairs.

In another variation from the dream, my dad was not at all happy with *Bisavó* going with us, but he clearly couldn't think of any remotely polite way to avoid it. She seemed to be on her best behavior, so I figured he might become more reconciled to it on the car ride down.

The first part of the trip was uneventful. Dad talked a little about the strangely sudden offer that had the firm scrambling to get him to Santa Brígida as soon as possible. He seemed to be buying it and was excited to be participating in an architectural renaissance in Santa Barbara, but I also had the feeling he was more or less flying on autopilot; his brain hadn't really caught up yet. Mom asked a few questions but seemed nervous. *Bisavó* made a point of saying little. Eventually even my dad's conversation faded away, and we rode on for a while in silence.

Dad had initially entertained the idea of having a late dinner in Santa Brígida, but traffic was heavier than we thought, and he finally suggested having dinner in San Luis Obispo, which we did, in a nice place relatively close to the coast. When I saw the place, I was glad he'd decided to take I-5 and US-101 instead of the much further inland CA-99S route, even though it was a little shorter.

When we sat down, I was shocked to see Tal, Alex and Khalid sitting in a booth across the restaurant.

"Be cool," Tal thought to me, *"Your dad doesn't know who we are and won't remember seeing us when we meet him officially later on. It's just harder to order food when you're invisible."* Well, I couldn't argue with that or begrudge them dinner after they were going so far out of their way to keep me safe.

I had really juicy pork chops, and they were excellent. By the time we finished, the sun had already set. By itself that wouldn't have spooked me, but the parking lot looked darker than it should have. The lights hadn't come on yet, even though I was sure it was more than dark enough to activate whatever lighting there was.

As we stepped out of the restaurant, I saw the broken glass in the parking lot.

Even more alarming, my dad suddenly slumped beside me, unconscious. The guys were coming out just behind us, and Alex caught him before he hit the ground.

"Sorry," Tal said.

"You did that?" I asked, uncertain how to react.

"Couldn't take the chance. We can't afford to have him see too much. You noticed the glass, right?"

"Yeah," I said. "Company?"

"Lots of it, I'm afraid. Looks as if they're waiting for us to step away from the light of the restaurant."

"Ma'am," said Tal, "there aren't too many people in the restaurant right now. Can you keep them occupied so *they* don't see anything?" *Bisavó* nodded and started to weave an illusion of some kind so that the customers and staff would see only an empty parking lot without battles to the death or supernatural fireworks.

"How did they find us?" I asked, noticing a little movement in the darkness around us.

"Dude, they must really, really want you," Tal said. "They've got to have had someone watching from every shadow between Madisonville and here. Tough to do, but if they put enough manpower into it, possible."

"The car's headlights are smashed too," said Alex, pointing with his sword.

"We can't drive off that way, and we can't exactly call the Auto Club at this point." Tal turned to my mom. "I'll open a portal big enough for the car, and you'll drive it through while we cover you."

"I'll do whatever it takes," said Mom. *Bisavó* must have told her enough to know that this was no ordinary sixteen-year-old giving her orders.

"I need to make some arrangements, though," Tal continued. "We can't have the car suddenly appear in Santa Brígida if there are witnesses around. I'll have to check the other side of the portal first."

"Do we have the time?" asked Mom worriedly.

"I think so, but just in case, can you and Lucas's…grandmother hold your husband? Khalid, Alex, can you take Lucas and fly him a little overhead? Keep him out of range until I get back. I just need a minute."

Without really waiting for a response, Tal opened a portal and stepped through it. *Bisavó* took Dad out of Alex's hands, and Alex and Khalid each grabbed one of mine. Then, making it look easy, they flew me into the air.

I felt a little like I had somehow drifted into a Peter Pan movie…well, except that Peter was looking for his shadow, and I was hoping to stay as far away from shadows as possible.

That would have worked a lot better if the shadows hadn't been able to fly.

The unnatural darkness flowed toward us. The problem was how to respond in our relatively awkward position. Khalid couldn't fire with at least one hand holding me up, and Alex could swing his sword clumsily at best. I wasn't exactly poised for any decent capoeira move either.

The guys made the only play they could. They landed. Alex, suddenly looking like a much more adept sword fighter, started swinging, and Khalid started shooting. Khalid's was the more effective tactic in this case, since each arrow hit generated one of those light producing explosions, but every shadow hit by Alex's sword vanished with a shriek. The shadows pressed closer though, and I knew it was only a matter of time before someone got stabbed and poisoned.

Tal popped back through the portal and looked at us in disbelief.

"They can fly!" shouted Khalid.

"We're abandoning the car, then," said Tal, drawing his sword in a flaming arc and using its blasts to push back the shadows. "Everyone through now! I'll cover you."

Tal was obviously a good strategist, and his plan might have worked too, except for one thing.

We had been assuming the shadows were all from human beings.

We were wrong.

As we moved toward the portal, a massive wave of shadow smashed into Tal's fire and pushed it back with such force that he only barely managed to avoid having all of us get roasted by the back blast.

We might still have been safe if we hadn't all frozen for a few seconds instead of making a run for the portal. Even Tal looked around desperately instead of heading toward safety, but he was more trying to figure out what the hell was going on than freezing.

When we finally got moving, we were too late. Another shadow blast hit the portal, and it dissolved in a shower of silver.

"Alex, Plan B!" yelled Tal. He tried shooting fire again, and again it was met with a shadow counterattack that quickly neutralized it. Khalid launched arrows into the darkness. They gave their usual satisfying explosion, but I could tell they weren't hitting the creature Tal was having trouble with.

It was further away…and much, much bigger.

I might have been able to sense more, but at that moment Alex grabbed me and took off.

"What the hell?" I said, squirming in his grasp.

"Stop struggling!" demanded Alex. "You'll just slow me down!"

"We're abandoning my parents!" I protested.

"No, we're not, but I have to concentrate…explain later." Alex was even more muscular than I had thought. He squeezed me until I felt as if my ribs would crack. I took the hint and stopped moving.

It didn't take me long to realize what the plan was. The big shadow, whatever it was, was following us! I guessed the idea was that Tal and Khalid could keep the others at bay, protecting my family and themselves.

Unfortunately the sandals of Hermes weren't really designed to fly two people, and I realized then why Alex had been so upset with my flailing around. Even with me immobile, the big thing was gaining on us. I couldn't feel any other shadows nearby, but that one seemed more than capable of finishing us.

"Family still safe," Alex muttered.

I wanted to ask how he knew but realized he was trying to focus all his attention on getting us wherever we were going in one piece.

Having nothing else to do, I tried to see how much I could sense about our pursuer. It was not a human shadow, and it was bigger than both of us put together. Beyond that, it was hard to tell.

Then a vision came to my aid. I saw a weird creature with the front claws and legs of a lion, the hind legs and head of a goat, and the tail of a snake. The image looked familiar, but English was never my best subject, so it took me a couple of minutes to realize what I was seeing was a chimera. That monster's shadow was what was chasing us!

I felt a momentary headache, as if my vision had gone into overdrive, and then I knew instinctively the serpent tail would have the same shadow poison that had almost killed me. However, that wasn't our biggest problem.

The mythical monster could breathe fire. Its shadow could apparently breathe darkness, and in bursts strong enough to disrupt magic and overwhelm fire and other light sources.

The Populus Umbrae had brought out the big guns.

Even as my vision-haunted brain was putting two and two together, a blast of the beast's breath narrowly missed us, and the ambient air temperature must have dropped twenty degrees. Great! One wrong move, and we'd be giant ice cubes.

Again I wished I could do something. Right now I was just dead weight, and if the creature caught up with Alex, it would be my fault.

Just in time, we reached what Alex's objective must have been: a large, well-lit shopping-mall parking lot. The chimera shadow might be way more powerful than a human shadow, but apparently even it couldn't fly into the light. It hunkered down right out of range of the parking-lot lighting, probably planning its next move.

"Everybody's safe back at the restaurant," Alex said, as soon as we landed.

"How do you know?" I looked warily at where I knew the shadow chimera was.

"I'm psychically linked to Tal," Alex explained. "He sort of networks us so he can communicate super-fast with us during combat. He thought maybe that would freak you out, so he didn't do it with you, but he's asking if he can include you now."

I nodded without hesitation, and I felt what must have been the psychic network reach out from Tal through Alex and engulf me. Suddenly I felt the presence, not only of Tal, but of Alex and Khalid in my head.

"You guys OK?" thought Tal.

"I'm fine, thanks to Alex," I thought back.

"It looks as if the chimera doesn't know what to do about the lights, just as I hoped. The creature never was that bright; I don't imagine its shadow is any better. Most of the other shadows have vanished, though, so I'm guessing they'll be along to start figuring ways to smash those lights any minute."

"You...you expected this?" I asked, amazed.

"Not even remotely," admitted Tal, *"but when Alex and I noticed the parking lot at the restaurant start to go dark, we worked out plan B. I have a few spy tricks, like being able to see through birds, so finding a well-lit place for Alex to fly you to just in case wasn't hard."*

I felt the night around us fill with shadows.

"Got an exit strategy? The rest of the shadow army is arriving," I pointed out.

"I'm going to open a portal for you in a minute. It'll be right in the middle of the lot."

At that moment, a blast of shadow shot from the chimera shadow and nearly hit us before it dissipated.

"Hurry!" I thought. My only answer was a kind of mental static. Apparently the chimera's blast took down the psychic network.

"That's bad!" said Alex, eyes darting back and forth. "Tal was going to use his connection with us to open the portal. He's never been here, so he can't open one to here without that kind of link. He'll have to fly here himself, and then open the portal. That'll take a few minutes."

The chimera shadow breathed on the light pole nearest to it. The shadowy breath quickly dissipated in the light, but the cold must have done something to the wiring, and that light winked out. The human shadows and the chimera one pressed closer and targeted the next-nearest light.

"A few minutes we may not have." I shivered a little despite myself as the air around us got colder.

"We could fly somewhere else, but we already know the chimera is faster, and I don't know what other nearby locations might work."

Another breath, and another light went down. This time the chimera aimed higher, and the cold shattered the glass and bulb.

"If the chimera gets too close, it'll just blast Tal's portal again if he opens one," Alex said, looking around for a way out.

The mall was basically an outdoor mall. We could have sought shelter inside one of the stores, but it would be only a matter of time before the chimera or one of the other shadows would figure out that breathing on the power lines might black out the whole place, and then we'd be done...maybe with a lot of innocent bystanders.

Somewhere in my head I felt Tal fighting chimera static in an effort to reestablish contact, but the creature must have sensed that. It fired at us each time, missing us but coming close enough to break the connection again.

I knew what I had to do.

"I'll draw them off," I said, my voice reflecting little of what I actually felt. "I can run fast, and we know for sure they'll follow. Then Tal can get you out."

Surprisingly, Alex laughed. "You just don't get it, do you? You're one of us now, at least if you want to be, and Tal would never leave you behind...I wouldn't either."

Another breath took out another light, and we shifted as far away from the shadows as we could get.

"I don't think I would do that for a complete stranger," I said. "Are you sure?"

"Dude, I'm a complete stranger to you, and you just basically offered to sacrifice yourself for me," Alex pointed out.

Weird! I hadn't thought about it at all until he pointed it out to me.

"If we could do something about the chimera shadow, we'd be able to hold out until Tal got here," Alex said wistfully, his sentence punctuated by the shattering of another light. This process was working far faster than having human shadows throw rocks at the lights.

"What does your…weapon do?" I asked. It was clearly a sword but had a curve like a sickle.

"Sorry, but no light effects. It does, though, cut anything. Apollo told me it was the same weapon Chronos used to overthrow Uranus, the same one Perseus used to cut off Medusa's head."

I didn't understand the first reference but got the second one.

A light popped from the cold and flickered out. We shifted positions again as we talked. Pretty soon we would be out of shifting room.

"It cuts even the shadows, forces them back to their world," Alex added. "Problem is, I can't see them. I have no way to aim it, and the chimera would freeze me or bite me with its tail if I got close without knowing what I was doing."

"I can see them," I said, considering possible strategies in my head. "At least, I can see enough of an outline to strike."

"But you can't fly," objected Alex.

"Ah, state-the-obvious night! I can run real fast, though, and the chimera's on the ground right now."

"If I let you do what I think you're suggesting, and it doesn't work, Tal will skin me alive and rub salt all over me," said Alex. "You can see the creatures, but you aren't used to fighting with weapons, and there are a lot of those assassins, I bet. Can you dodge all of the ones in between and get to the chimera before it ices you?"

I shook my head slowly. Alex was right; that plan sucked. However, there was one other possibility. I put both hands on his head.

"Trying a mind meld, are we?" he said humorlessly.

"Shut up!" I responded. He did, though we had to shuffle away from the growing darkness. We were down to very few lights in the parking lot now. I heard breaking glass and knew some shadows were on the other side, breaking the lights outside each store in the mall.

Yeah, it was borderline crazy to try to establish a mental link with Alex, but the idea had two things going for it. We were already part of a network, and, though it was disrupted, I still felt some connection.

We were right next to each other, touching skin to skin, which ought to count for something in terms of overcoming the static—or so I hoped. I knew nothing about how magic worked except for the little I had learned today, but my instinctive responses had been good so far.

Also, I was part Encantado, and apparently part xana as well. I might not be a natural mind reader, but at least some of my ancestors' powers were mental, and my visions and intuitions suggested I might have inherited enough to use a preexisting mental connection.

Anyway, crazy idea or not, we were not exactly blessed with a wealth of choices.

Tal and Khalid arrived at that point, but there wasn't going to be a quick portal rescue. The chimera shadow turned on them, and it was all Tal could do to keep them from dying right then. Besides, the chimera breath they were dodging once again kept him from connecting with us. I hoped it wouldn't keep me from connecting with Alex though.

Just as I was about to give up, I felt a little click in my head, and I sensed Alex's presence, though it was weaker than before.

"Is the connection good enough for you to see through my eyes?" I asked.

"I've done that with Tal when we're connected," replied Alex. "Uh, yeah. The perspective shift is awkward, but I can make out where the chimera is, and its back is to me. I can probably hit it from the air. Worth a try anyway!"

Alex took off, flying much faster when not burdened with me. The other shadows might have blocked him, but they, like the chimera, were focused on Tal and must not have realized what Alex was doing until it was too late.

Somewhat awkwardly, Alex oriented himself over the chimera, and then dropped, slashing wildly. My position was so different from his that he still couldn't aim well, but, through my eyes, he could see his approximate position in relation to the chimera, and his sword strokes had such strength that he was bound to hit something. He aimed well enough to slice off that snake tail.

The beast screamed, but it was strong enough to resist immediate banishment. However, as Alex descended, he kept hacking away with such ferocity that in no time his curved blade ripped into the creature's hybrid body, tearing chunks out and flinging them all over the place. It could resist that treatment for only seconds.

Alex, surrounded by other shadows, might have died at that point, but with the chimera gone, Tal was able to light the area with fire. It wasn't as effective as the sunlight from Gordy's sword, but it was enough to send the shadows running again. Those that were inclined to stay as close as they could were dissuaded by a few shots from Khalid's bow. As soon as I could see it was clear, I ran over to them at top speed.

Against all odds, we had won again. I wouldn't have appreciated the magnitude of it, numb as I was, if Tal hadn't been so excited by it.

"Great job, Alex," he said, slapping him on the back.

"Couldn't have done it without Lucas." Alex pointed at me with his sword—really not the best habit, but, at this point, I didn't mind.

"He revived the psychic connection between us enough to let me see through his eyes, or I could never have hit the chimera like that," Alex explained.

Tal looked at me and whistled in appreciation. "So speed and precognition are not the only abilities you have? Wow, even a bigger freak than you thought." I must have looked downcast, because Tal added, "Joking. Nobody's a freak, remember?" Then he slapped me on the back.

"My family?" I asked, looking around.

"Already in Santa Brígida, where it's high time we joined them," Tal replied, starting to open a portal. It took him much longer than before, and, as I watched his face in its silver light, I realized how tired he really was. He was, in fact, barely standing.

None of us needed to be asked twice. We passed briefly to Alcina's island, whose daylight blinded me, and, from there, to the comparative darkness of a street in what must have been Santa Brígida.

"We've lost them," Tal announced, looking around. "Unless they overheard our conversation at some point, they don't know where Lucas is right now.

"You know," he continued, "I should have put your dad to sleep and done this in the first place. I underestimated how fast the Populus Umbrae would catch up with you."

I noticed Viviane standing nearby. I greeted her, but Tal corrected me automatically. "Refer to her as Nurse Florence."

"She looks younger than she is," he explained. "She's the school nurse, and—"

"What?" I asked quietly. "Every guy in school must end up in the nurse's office!"

Tal chuckled. "Yeah, pretty much, and the job was really a cover for her to keep watch on me, before I had discovered the true extent of my...situation. She takes the role seriously though. Even I don't get to call her Viviane in public. I suppose I could in private, but I've never really thought about it."

"Sorry," I said. "I'll be more careful."

"Nurse Florence, are the protections in place?" Tal asked.

"Everything Carla, Vanora, and I could put together," she replied. "Lucas's house has as much protection on it as yours, and the Populus Umbrae shouldn't be able to come through anywhere within the town limits. At night, Lucas will have to stay in town, and preferably in the house for a few days, but considering how little time we had, I think we made pretty good arrangements."

"What are we going to do with Lucas's father when we wake him up?" asked Mom.

"The situation seems more difficult than when I put him to sleep in Madisonville," said *Bisavó*, "but I will try to construct an appropriate dream."

"I'll take care of it, ma'am," said Tal. "It's easier to craft a false memory that will fool a person if you can read the person's mind."

"I have never known any being who could actually read minds," said *Bisavó*, this time more in wonder than in skepticism.

"It's rare, though I think more could learn it if they thought about it," said Tal. "The limits of magic are a function of the worldview of the spell caster." I must have looked confused, because he turned to me and said, "Think about it. How many myths or even fairy tales involve mind reading? Not a whole lot. Ancient casters, and even many modern ones, just never visualized it. Nor did I in my earlier lives, but I could train myself to do it."

Tal got to work, so that by the time my dad awakened, he would remember the car breaking down in San Luis Obispo, Carrie Winn sending a limo to pick us up, and yet another person to handle the car. That story necessitated Tal retrieving our luggage from the car though. I thought he should just leave it alone, tired as he was, but Viviane—uh—Nurse Florence went with him to do the portals, and they returned with our stuff in about three minutes.

"Explaining why the car wasn't here was easy, but I couldn't think of a good excuse to explain the absence of your luggage," he said. "No shadows to deal with either. So far, they only show up when you're around."

The implication of "so far" wasn't lost on me. If they couldn't get me, would the shadows start coming after my new friends…or my old ones, for that matter?

By the time Tal finished crafting the false memory and revived my dad, "Carrie Winn" was there to greet him, thank him profusely for coming, and give us all a tour of our house—which conveniently happened to be the one we were standing in front of. Tal and the others quickly made themselves scarce, but not before Tal drew me aside long enough to let me relink to him.

"I'm not going to rummage around in your mind," Tal assured me. "The link gives you an ability to send me a distress call if you need to, and, similarly, I can send you a warning if one is needed."

Our house was not the palace in our dream, but it was bigger than the place in Madisonville, and my dad was impressed with the design. I wasn't as concerned about that as I was the fact that the place felt natural, as if I really belonged. The Madisonville house was always just a house. Somehow, I knew this one would be a home.

And if that night I slept with a night light for the first time since I was about six, who could blame me?

Chapter 10: Postlude (Umbra)

I knew I was chained, but I didn't care. Chained was better than dead…maybe. Never having been dead, I wasn't sure.

The chain prevented me from using magic, and I felt naked without the shadows. Extra light sources had been brought in, wiping away any trace of shadow anywhere close to me. Well, almost any. She who devised this imprisonment may not have thought about the fact that my body threw a shadow, but it didn't matter. I kept looking into it but saw nothing. Perhaps the chain kept the Praeceptor or anyone else from knowing where I was. Without having a feeling about which shadow to look through, no one would ever find me.

Did I want anyone to find me? They would probably kill me if they took me back, but perhaps not. I might be forgiven if I found a way to complete my mission.

Whether or not I wanted to be forgiven was the biggest question.

In some ways, I was more like the beings who had captured me than I was like the Populus Umbrae. Was I truly human myself? Would I like to live as a human?

Would I even be permitted to live as a human, or would I always live in this cell, with lights so bright I kept imagining my skin burning away?

Even if I was permitted to leave this prison, could I learn how to be human?

Killing was all I knew. Was it all I could ever know?

The Adventure Isn't Over

If you liked this novel, you might also like the other volumes in the Spell Weaver series, also available from Amazon.

"Echoes from My Past Lives" is a short prequel that tells the story of Tal's original transformation. Find out how his past lives first became a part of his present one...and how that process nearly cost him his life.

Living with Your Past Selves, the first book in the series, picks up Tal's life four years after "Echoes from My Past Lives" ends and a short time before *Divided among Yourselves* begins. Having managed to survive the avalanche of past life memories, Tal pulls himself together and makes good use of the lessons learned and skills developed in those previous lives. He still has the ability to work magic, and there is no denying that's cool. No, his life isn't perfect, but he is managing.

However, his best friend, Stan, has begun to suspect his secret, and Stan isn't the only one. Suddenly, Tal is under attack from a mysterious enemy and under the protection of an equally mysterious friend whose agenda Tal can't quite figure out. An apparition predicts his death. A shape shifter disguised as Stan attacks him. An old adversary starts acting like a friend. He and some other students get hurled into Annwn (the Otherworld), face Morgan le Fay, and only just barely get back alive--and that's just during the first month of school!

By now Tal knows he is not the only one who can work magic and certainly not the only one who can remember the past. He realizes there is something that he is not remembering, something that could save his life or end it, some reason for the attacks on him that, as they escalate, threaten not only him but everyone he loves as well. In an effort to save them, he will have to risk not only his life, but even his soul.

Divided against Yourselves, the second novel in the series, picks up Tal's story within days of the end of *Living with Your Past Selves.* Tal thought that he had saved himself and his friends when he defeated the witch Ceridwen. He was wrong.

He always thought of evil as embodied in external threats that he could overcome in combat. Soon he will discover that the worst evil has been inside of him all along....

Tal's girlfriend is in a coma for which he holds himself responsible. A close friend, suffering from a past-life memory trauma similar to Tal's, is getting worse, not better. Morgan le Fay is still lurking around and has an agenda Tal can't figure out. Supernatural interruptions in his life are becoming more frequent, not less so, despite his expectations. In fact, Tal learns that something about his unique nature amplifies otherworldly forces in ways he never imagined were possible, ways that place at risk everyone close to him.

Tal and his allies must face everything from dead armies to dragons. As soon as they overcome one menace, another one is waiting for them. More people are depending on Tal than ever; he carries burdens few adults could face, let alone a sixteen-year-old like himself. Yet somehow Tal at first manages to handle everything the universe throws at him.

What Tal can't handle is the discovery that a best friend, almost a brother, betrayed him, damaging Tal's life beyond repair. For the first time, Tal feels a darkness within him, a darkness which he can only barely control...assuming he wants to. He's no longer sure. Maybe there is something to be said for revenge, and even more to be said for taking what he wants. After all, he has the power...

Hidden among Yourselves, the third novel in the series, picks up shortly after the ending of *Divided among Yourselves*. Tal faces more challenging mysteries than he has ever dealt with before. Unfortunately, solving them means the difference between life and death—and not just for Tal.

He must find out why the spirit of murder is stalking the people of Santa Brígida. He must find out why a war god wants him dead. To keep a powerful enemy from going free, he must find and retrieve an ancient artifact from a realm he did not believe existed, a realm which he cannot enter, and which none of the inhabitants can leave. Along the way he must also try to figure out if one of his friends is really Alexander the

Great reincarnated, how someone could be spontaneously resurrected, and whether a madman is really as mad as he seems.

As if these mysteries were not enough, Tal must also confront opponents stronger than ever, armies of them...and this time they aren't going to take prisoners. Not only that, but another one of Tal's friends will betray him, and in a way that will make the earlier betrayal seem like an act of kindness.

"Destiny or Madness" is a paraquel to *Hidden among Yourselves* that looks at the events in Chapter 2 of that work from Alex's point of view.

Alex is on the verge of getting what he always wanted: a chance to escape from his dull life and enter the world of Greek mythology. Unfortunately, he also discovers the truth of the old saying, "Be careful what you wish for, because you might get it!"

Tasked by Ares, the god of war, with killing one of his fellow students, Alex questions his own sanity. That's just the beginning of Alex's problems, though. Now trapped in a struggle between supernatural forces he can't begin to understand and forced to use a weapon that is really using him, Alex's only escape may be to find the love that has eluded him his whole life.

Evil within Yourselves, the fourth book in the series, begins shortly after the ending of *Hidden among Yourselves.* Taliesin Weaver has survived attack by vindictive witches, ferocious dragons, scheming faerie kings, and even angry ex-gods. Unfortunately, his enemies have not given up, and now they are scheming to destroy the foundation on which his success has been built: his friends.

One by one the people closest to Tal fall for tricks that lure them out of town, leaving them—and him—more vulnerable to attack. Even worse, some of them unwittingly succumb to temptations that tie them to Tal's worst enemies and set them up to fail Tal when he needs them most.

Tal can no longer rely on his friends. Worse, he can't even rely on himself. Unaware that the girl he thinks he loves has cast a spell on him, Tal finds himself having more and more trouble containing Dark Me, the evil alter ego that now wrestles him daily for control of his body. That situation is bad enough to begin with, but when a misguided faerie spell gives Dark Me a body and makes him indistinguishable from Tal by any means, scientific or magical, all Hell breaks loose—literally!

Other short Spell Weaver works, including the short story, "Angel Feather" will be released in the next few months, so be sure to watch for them.

If you like to read in other genres, you might enjoy my essay, **"Sea of Dreams,"** available in the anthology, ***Where Dreams and Visions Live***. If you are a parent with a high school age son or daughter and have not always had success interacting with teachers, you might be interested in the booklet, **"A Parent's Guide to Parent-Teacher Communication."**
About the Author

About the Author

As soon as he learned to read, Bill Hiatt loved reading. Just as kids who are passionate sports fans often want to be athletes, kids who are passionate readers often want to be writers, and so it was with Bill. Though he dreamed of many career paths over the years, two remained while others came and went: teaching and writing. Fortunately for the world, there was no such thing as self-publishing when Bill was in college and writing horrendous love poetry. Luckily, he kept trying other genres, and he kept reading. He also graduated from UCLA with a degree in English and went on to pursue one of his two dreams by teaching English, mostly at the high school level, for thirty-six years.

Teaching was far more than a day job for Bill; it was his life. He had thought originally that he might be able to both teach and write, but the demands of teaching caused him to forget about writing…for a while. Then, one day Bill, trying to write an interesting grammar test, created one in narrative form, a short story about the students in that particular class. He got so wrapped up in it that he stayed up almost all night writing it. The students loved the test, demanded more like it, and scored better in grammar than any group Bill had ever taught. That experience made Bill realized that he hadn't really abandoned being a writer; he had merely postponed it. He found time to publish a little at the end of his teaching career. Now that he is retired, all the stories accumulated somewhere in the back of his mind will finally be able to get out.

If you would like more information about Bill, this novel, and/or his other writing projects, you can visit him at http://billhiatt.com/, at his author page on Facebook (http://www.facebook.com/#!/pages/Bill-Hiatt/431724706902040/), and on Twitter (https://twitter.com/BillHiatt2). In the first two locations, you can sign up for his mailing list, so that you can be the first to hear about giveaways, new releases, and other cool stuff.

Made in United States
North Haven, CT
03 September 2024

56931540R00065